KYAN GREEN

AND THE INFINITY RACERS

COLM FIELD

Illustrated by **DAVID WILKERSON**

BLOOMSBURY
CHILDREN'S BOOKS
LONDON OXFORD NEW YORK NEW DELHI SYDNEY

BLOOMSBURY CHILDREN'S BOOKS
Bloomsbury Publishing Plc
50 Bedford Square, London WC1B 3DP, UK
29 Earlsfort Terrace, Dublin 2, Ireland

BLOOMSBURY, BLOOMSBURY CHILDREN'S BOOKS and the Diana logo
are trademarks of Bloomsbury Publishing Plc

First published in Great Britain in 2023 by Bloomsbury Publishing Plc

A catalogue record for this book is available from the British Library

ISBN: PB: 978-1-5266-4174-8; eBook: 978-1-5266-4173-1

2 4 6 8 10 9 7 5 3 1

Typeset by RefineCatch Limited, Bungay, Suffolk

Printed and bound in Great Britain by CPI Group (UK) Ltd, Croydon CR0 4YY

To find out more about our authors and books visit www.bloomsbury.com
and sign up for our newsletters

To D and the kids

1

We found the Infinite Race on the first day of the summer holidays, when we were helping my dad plug leaks in the roof.

Well, I say *we* found – my sister Celestine swears she saw it first. But all she did was point at an old box, which my grandma would say is like finding a mouldy sandwich in your room and saying you invented penicillin. And I say *we* were helping, but while *I* had the vital job of holding the second torch to make sure Dad didn't put his foot through the ceiling, Celestine had been told to stay on the floor below us and 'foot the ladder', which if you ask me is one of those jobs you ask a little kid to do so they feel *involved*. Like drawing a smiley picture of the sun, or

1

seeing if they can be quiet for ten whole minutes.

Anyway, so Dad was stomping around the loft, grunting, grumbling and spraying more foam than a fire extinguisher. I was sat in the hatch, legs resting on the ladder, aiming the torch at him and thinking about how my best friend Luke was probably playing on some shiny new console while I was having to 'earn' half an hour on my tired old tablet. And then, suddenly, Celestine pointed up past me, and said, 'What's that, Ky?'

(Just to be clear: if I say that Tines said, 'What's that, Ky?' what she *actually* said was, 'What's that, Ky? Kyan, what's that? Let me see, Kyan. Kyan? Kyan. Ky? What's that? Ky, what's . . . ?')

I looked nervously around the dark, cobwebby loft. There were at least fifty bags and boxes, all shapes and sizes, all covered in dust. Mum says everyone who rented this flat before us left things here, but our landlord Mr Stringer won't let us throw them out. The first time I came up here, I loved the treasure I found. *A globe! Trading cards that nobody's ever heard of!* But then I found this weird home-made Princess Elsa doll that gave me nightmares for weeks.

'Actually, Tines,' I said importantly, trying to ignore Elsa's freakily human hair sticking out of a black bag by the crumbling brick wall, 'my job is quite important you know, and . . .'

And then I caught a glimpse of the box Celestine was pointing at, sticking out of a bag that was just behind me. On the side of it was a picture of something that makes every kid's heart soar. It was a racetrack.

OK, so maybe a hundred years ago it would've made every kid's heart soar. Oranges were big news back then, according to school, so a racetrack would've been the real deal. Still, I had nothing better to do, so I shone the torch at it.

'Where's the light gone?' Dad yelled, and there was a thud. He said a word we weren't supposed to say, and I shone the torch back on him. There was dirt on his face and he was rubbing his head.

'You sweared,' I said.

'No I didn't,' he replied. 'And you weren't shining the torch anyway.' We looked at each other for a moment, stuck in a shotgun stand-off nobody could win. Then Dad disappeared, *pfft-pfft-pfft*ing with his expanding foam to the other end of the loft. Still sitting, I fixed the torch under my leg so that it stayed pointed at him, turned around, and hefted the racetrack over my shoulder, on to my lap.

3

It was in an old box, older than the board games we get from the charity shop where the kids on the cover are dressed like Peter Rabbit. This box was brown cardboard, and somebody had *drawn* the racetrack on it. It wasn't scrawled on though – not all messily, like if I'd done it. This road was a thick, black tarmac that looked solid and neat until I looked closer, and saw it was in fact made up of hundreds – no, *thousands* – of these tiny squiggly shapes, all clustered tightly together. The road carried on along the base of the box and up the sides.

I turned the box over, and saw that travelling along this road were all kinds of cars, lorries, even helicopters. They raced up and around the lid of the box, then as the racetrack continued around the other side, they dissolved into tiny squiggly shapes once again, above letters printed out like flames . . .

'*The Infinite Race*,' I read. 'Sounds lame.' But still, I balanced the box on the edge of the hatch and lifted the lid.

Beneath the instruction sheet was a stack of black racing track pieces, not that different from Scalextric except that they were made of metal instead of plastic. I lifted out the top piece, and saw that it had a chequerboard at one end, like the finish line for a race. At the other end, *stuck* to it, was a metal racecar. It looked old; *old*-old, the kind of car there'd only be black-and-white videos of.

'C'mon, let me seeeeee!' Celestine whined from the bottom of the ladder, and I was just about to let her. I really was. But then Dad called out, and I told her to wait by pointing at her the way I saw a bus driver do to Mum once, just before she shouted at him.

'You'll have to shine the torch down here, Ky,' said Dad. 'The hubcap transformer is sticking to the elephant's trunk and I have to regenerate.'

Actually, he *didn't* say that, but that's the kind of nonsense I hear when Dad tells me to do anything to help him fix up the flat. So I put the piece of track back in the box, stood up, and shone the torch in his general direction.

'Not there, the bacon-foil relay! George Foreman setting!'

I moved the torch again, and Dad gave a thumbs up. I sat back down, turned back . . . and nearly fell through the hatch.

Celestine wasn't footing the ladder.

Celestine was at the top of the ladder.

'Whaddya doing? Get out of my face!' I whispered, flinching back.

5

'I wanna l-o-o-k,' Celestine whined. All of a sudden she snatched at the track piece I was holding, and we had a mini tug-of-war right on that ladder, me clinging to the chequerboard end, Celestine gripping the end with the car on it.

'Not yet! Go back down, Dad'll go mad! Stop! Celestine, STOP!'

'I'd best not hear you two fighting!' Dad warned from the dark. I froze. Celestine ducked down.

'Er, no, Dad,' I said.

'The same goes for later. I don't want to hear about trouble from your grandma, and I *really* don't want any trouble if you come back before Mr Stringer's visit.'

'Yes, Dad!' we both said.

'Although to be honest, I really *don't* want you back here till he's gone,' Dad added. 'That's why your grandma's taking you to the park. You know what he's like about kids.'

'And humans,' I added. I don't like the way Mum and Dad sound nervous when they talk about Mr Stringer, especially when he's so rude to them.

'Did you really nearly call him Mr Stringybum last time, Dad?' Celestine said.

Dad cackled.

'Yeah, don't go putting that in my head.'

Dad went off spraying foam again. After a moment, Celestine climbed back up, and we kept fighting more quietly, like he'd asked.

'It's mine!'

'Get down before—'

'I saw it first!'

'You'll drop it.'

'I won't drop it!'

'You'll drop it, now get *off*—'

CRACK.

It happened as soon as Celestine grabbed the metal car. I felt a shock of electricity up my arms, and let go. There was this moment of pure terror as I saw Celestine's face widen in surprise and thought *No no NO, she's going to fall!* But she didn't, not yet. I looked up at her, and saw to my amazement that her thick cornrows were standing up on end, uncurling before my eyes, and just as everything seemed to *sloooooooow doooowwwwwn*, I smelt it.

'*Eeeeeeeeeeuuuuuuuuuuuuuuuwwwwwwwwww*,' I said. '*Wwwhaaaaat's thaaaaaat ponnng?*'

'*Smelllllllt iiiit, deallllllllllt iiiit,*' Celestine began to say back, but then she gasped, and looked past me. As she did, I heard the roar of a crowd, an impossible crowd standing in an impossible breeze that lifted the hairs on my arms,

7

beneath the warmth of a sun I could feel but not see, and . . .

'*Looooook—*' Celestine began to shout. I heard the *vvoomVoomVOOM!* of a powerful engine right behind me, and Celestine *did* start to fall back, and without another thought I grabbed out at her, knocking the car from her hand . . .

'OUT!' Celestine finished, and time returned. There was the clatter of the metal racecar tumbling down the ladder, slapping the floor and rolling away out of sight.

Then there was silence. I sat there, holding on to Celestine's T-shirt, breathing hard. The breeze faded, and her hair fell back down, untied, messy.

'Did you *see* that?' Celestine squeaked. I shook my head. I'd heard it though. A crowd, a car. I'd felt it too. A sun, a breeze. And I'd smelt it, a smell that I could place now. It was burning rubber, the smell our car made for a while last year.

It was the smell of a race. An impossible race. I was about to say *how* impossible it had to be when I saw Dad *stomp-stomp* out of the dark, a thunderous expression on his face.

'KYAN, WHY DID YOU LET CELESTINE UP THE LADD-ARGH!'

CRUNCH.

That was the sound of my dad's foot going through the ceiling.

2

'No, no, no no no no, Grandma, it's *magic*, like *proper magic*! We picked it up, and a RACECAR went *WHOOOOSH* through the house! Kyan, tell her – NO, NO, WAIT – we picked up the track and the RACECAR went *ZZZZZOOOOOM* and I smelt this burned fart smell and . . . OW!'

We were sitting on a bench opposite the park. Unfortunately for Celestine, before we'd made it inside, Grandma had seen her friend from church, Christine. As soon as Christine called to us from over by the swings, Grandma had looked at my sister's untidy cornrows and dragged us back over the road to re-plait them.

'Oh Celestine, hush,' Grandma said. 'What were you

'thinking, untying them in the first place?'

'I *didn't*, Grandma, that's what I'm *trying to tell you*! It was the car! The fart smell . . . OW!'

'*Enough* with all these curse words!' Grandma said, and yanked three fronds apart as she said it, glancing to see if her friend was watching. Fortunately Christine was beaming through thick-rimmed glasses at her baby grand-daughter, her green dangly earrings waving back and forth as she clapped her hands.

'What curse words?' Celestine continued foolishly, and laughed like she always does, right at the wrong time.

'*Fart?* Ha-ha-ha . . . OW! Tell her, Ky! Tell her about *Infant Race!*'

'Racing infants?' Grandma frowned. 'You can't do that. What's this all about, Kyan?'

The trouble is, Celestine's only eight. She didn't realise that what she *thought* she saw two hours ago was impossible. I'm ten. I could see it all clearly. Hair *doesn't* undo itself. Toys *aren't* magic. Invisible racecars *don't* rocket through leaky lofts. Whatever had happened up in the attic, we'd imagined it, and even if we hadn't, no grown-up was ever going to believe us. So I put on a cheesy, patient, big-brother grin, and lied my socks off.

'Not racing infants!' I laughed airily. '*The Infinite Race!* It's just a toy we found! Celestine's got an overactive imagination, you know. It did have really great sound effects though!'

'Just a toy,' Grandma repeated, studying my face. 'How would a toy undo her hair? Why would a toy make your dad put his foot through the ceiling on the day *that* wretched man is visiting your flat?'

'I really don't know,' I said, smiling so wide I could taste earwax. 'But you're doing Tines's hair now, and Dad said he's hoping Mr Stringer doesn't notice the ceiling before he has the chance to fix it. It almost . . . doesn't matter?'

Celestine's eyes narrowed with anger the same time as Grandma's narrowed with suspicion. I wondered how both my eight-year-old little sister and my hundred-year-old Grandma could terrify me with just a look.

'Well, good,' Grandma said finally, and folded Celestine's hair into a clip like a magic trick. 'If it's just a racetrack, you two can build it when we get back.'

'My tablet time . . .' I began to protest, but Grandma's an evil genius when it comes to distracting us. She got up and played one of the songs I'd put on her phone, the one I *love* that she can't hear the naughty words to. Soon me and Celestine were bobbing our heads and our hands like MCs, the sun shining down on us. A car full of teenagers drove past, playing the *same* song and giving us props. Celestine grinned at me, and I was about to grin back, when I heard Luke's voice.

'Kyan! It's Kyan!'

I laughed. My gang were peering through the park fence, daft grins on their faces. There was Dimitar and Stefania, the twins who're proper different – like, Stef is as blunt as a brick to the head and always bangs on about her beloved science podcasts, while Dimi talks like an OG and lives for sports and Romanian rap, but they're both my friends and going round their flat is sweet because their mum's favourite English word is 'Cake?' And there was Luke too, my best mate forever, who *still* shouts my name when he sees me like I've just come back from space. I raced up to the zebra crossing, did a silly dance that had them in stitches, and thought, *There's nowhere in the world like home. Nowhere in the universe. Nowhere in a million universes.*

Funny thing, when I glanced back, Celestine looked disappointed. I wish I could say that I guessed why, but I didn't really think about it at all.

'I don't understand why you don't just *come*,' Luke said, one eye closed and his tongue sticking out as he aimed a long, skinny branch at the blue shopping tub balanced precariously up the tree in front of us. The branch prodded the tub, and snapped.

'Frankie's Football Factory costs *money*, Luke,' I said, looking around for something to throw. 'I can't go!' Honestly, he's my bestest friend, but when it comes to things he can have that I can't, Luke is *slow* to catch up. I found a meatier-looking stick, and lobbed it at our target. It crashed through branches, knocked out a few undergrown spiky conkers, and dropped uselessly back to the ground.

'Kyan!' Grandma's voice hollered at me from across the

park, and I winced. 'Why you throwing sticks like some kinda thug?!'

'Sorry, Grandma!' I shouted back. For one dread second I thought she'd walk over and start hectoring my friends, but then her friend Christine piped up, her jangly bracelets and crucifix swinging like weapons as she turned away to *her* grandson.

'And you, Tyrese! You're playin' too rough with Celestine, y'know!'

I mean, that wasn't true – the best thing for Tyrese to do was run away before my sister got wound up, but at least it moved Grandma and Christine's game of *Who's the Strictest Grandma?* back to the kids' end of the park.

It was Stefania who'd spotted the blue shopping tub high up in the tree, and after we'd started to guess what was hidden inside it – because why would you put it up there if it wasn't valuable or dangerous or both? – she'd got that fixed look in her eye that meant we would not be leaving this park until we found out.

'If somebody runs into the tree hard enough ...' Stefania was saying now, looking thoughtfully at me. I took half a step back.

'I don't want to go to football camp on my own.' Luke was still moaning.

'Er, Luke—' began Dimitar.

'It's Frankie's Football Factory, Luke!' I interrupted him. 'They have real players coaching there – you have to go!'

'Or catapult something *into* the tree. Like a *human-y* thing,' Stefania mused. Luke edged one step away.

'Luke,' Dimitar tried again. 'Me and Stef were—'

'You'll enjoy it when you're there, Luke,' I said. 'Remember what you said about Charades Club. Then you—'

'I don't *want* any more clubs,' Luke moaned. 'I already have origami on Wednesdays and drama on Fridays and pogo jumping on Sunday mornings, and next week I'm map reading – *map reading!* – and—'

'Hmm, *pogo* jumping,' said Stefania. 'With the right angle . . .' Both me and Luke took *another* step back.

'Luke, will you just listen?!' Dimi snapped. 'Our mum said yes. *We're* going to Football Factory.'

Luke leaped in the air with a 'Yippeeeeee!' and as they all started talking at once, about how great it would be and who would score the most goals, and even though two seconds ago I'd been the one telling Luke he should go, a queasy feeling began to grow inside my belly. Frankie's Football Factory is *amazing* – *two* weeks of proper football

16

training on *twenty* pitches, all ages getting coached by coaches and players from *real* teams.

And, as Dad likes to say, 'You need a footballer's wage to afford it!' For the past two years I had *begged* Mum and Dad to let me go, and for the past two years they'd said that they were really sorry, but they didn't love me enough. I'm kidding, of course. They just couldn't afford it. But now my friends would be there, all of them, for a big two-week chunk of the summer holidays, and I wouldn't.

It must've shown in my face, because Dimi looked at me, concerned.

'Hey, you sure you can't persuade your—'

'His mum and dad can't afford it this year, Dimi.' Stefania cut him off. She didn't mean it harshly, Stef just says things how they are, but that *hurt*.

'It's fine!' I said, covering. 'And Stef's right. Honestly. It's good you'll get to team up.'

But it wasn't good. It wasn't fine.

Just then, I felt a little-sister tap on my back, and turned.

'Be careful, Kyan!' Celestine said, loud enough for Grandma to hear. 'Don't throw sticks!'

'I'm *being* careful. Go away.' But she barely heard me. Her eyes kept glancing to my mates and back to me, like she was torn between ruining my fun and trying to impress them. And then she found a way to do both.

'Did you tell them about the *Infinite Race*?' She whispered it, and – *sheesh!* – her whispers are louder than some people's screams. My ears started to heat up the way they always do when I'm embarrassed. Imaginary games are fine for her, but right then for me it was just tragic. *You guys go to Football Factory, I'm just going to play racecars with my kid sister.*

'Not now, Tines.'

'What *magic* do you think it was—?'

'Go AWAY!' I said. It came out louder than I meant. Meaner too.

'Hey! Hey hey hey hey hey!' Grandma said, clicking her fingers at me, before she turned back to check if Christine had seen her finger-clicking Special Combo.

'I was just asking,' Celestine said to me in a hurt voice, and ran off.

'Tch! Kids, eh?' I said. The others nodded sympathetically.

'*What* race?' Dimi said, and somehow that was the thing that did it. Suddenly I felt a flash of anger, at my friends, at Frankie's Football Factory, at Mum and Dad, at my interfering sister. I grabbed the biggest log I could

19

manage, and lobbed it up in the air with all my strength, right up at the shopping tub in the tree.

It was a good shot. The tub fell back, dropped, smashed into a branch, and tipped forward over me.

You know if you see a big box in a tree the day after it's been raining? Don't try knocking it down. Why? Because you know what's in it, right? No? Well, let me tell you. Leaves, bugs, bird poo and a *lot* of water, that's what.

'Silly boy and your silly games!' scolded Grandma as she opened the front door. I hurried past her up the stairs, too busy shaking with wet and cold to answer. 'We weren't supposed to be back here until—'

A voice at the top of the stairs interrupted her. It was a haughty voice, a Disney villain's voice. A tall, thin frame loomed over the top of the stairs, and my heart sank. It was Mr Stringer.

'These walls look tired, Cynthia,' he said sharply. 'I hope you've been washing them as it specifies in the contract. What are these bumps, wall scabies?'

'That's your woodchip, Mr Stringer,' Mum said. 'We keep everything clean, although with children—'

'With children you can't afford to pay more rent, is that it?' Mr Stringer snapped. 'I'm losing a fortune on this place, you know. Have you any idea what I'm charging around the corner?'

'Mr Stringer,' Dad said, sounding like he'd been locked in the toilet for a week and the flush was broken. 'We look after this flat. I've been fixing holes in the roof just today, and—'

'AND the floors!' Mum said quickly, before Mr Stringer could look up at the foot-shaped hole in the ceiling.

'Holes in the *floors*?' Mr Stringer said, looking down, bemused.

It was bad luck that I chose that moment to take a step back down. My trainer squelched, and Mr Stringer looked down at my drenched appearance like he'd just swallowed off-food.

He was a tall man, with a stiff way of standing, like those cheap superhero toys where you can only move their head. His hair was always too gelled, and his shirts *too* bright, like he wasn't trying to seem cheerful so much as hoping to hurt your eyes.

'It's your son,' Mr Stringer said thinly, clearly hoping they'd say I wasn't, so he could call the police.

'Kyan,' Dad said. 'What the blummin' heck happened?' I saw panic in his face and realised I was making this whole situation *worse*. Desperately I searched for something to say, something funny and brilliant that would make Mr Stringer laugh. But before I could speak, Celestine ran up the stairs behind me.

'Hey, Mr Stringybum,' she said. 'You're beneath the big hole!'

It was a bad time for her to use the nickname we have for Mr Stringer. It was an even worse time for a piece of Dad's expanding foam to fall from the roof, through the boot-shaped hole in the ceiling, and float down gently on to Mr Stringer's nose.

3

'I meanNGRHGHBL ... what didYBDRYBDRGR ...
you *think*FLNBLNFBR ... would happen?!' I said
to Celestine between the hurricane that was Grandma
towel-drying my hair.

Celestine bit her lip and pretended to be interested in
the Infinite Race box. I could see she felt bad, but I was so
angry.

I honestly thought Mr Stringer would make us
move out right then and there. Luckily he had other
flats to visit, plus he spotted Grandma standing at the
bottom of the stairs with a warning frown you couldn't
have turned upside down with a string and a hook.
Instead, my dad dashed out to get supplies for the hole

in the ceiling, Mum took a last-minute shift at work to help pay for them, and our landlord promised to return later *to discuss restitution*, which Grandma said means he's looking to bleed more money out of them. Sometimes I wish her explanations were a bit more child-friendly.

'Mr Stringybum!' I exclaimed. 'You actually *called* him Mr Stringybum! To his face!'

'You're the one who got the carpet all soggy,' Celestine retorted. 'We wouldn't've even been home if you hadn't knocked that big tub over.'

'*Yeah*, but, *but* . . .' I started, realising, annoyingly, that she was right. '*Bu-ut – to his face!* And you told him about the hole in the ceiling!'

'Are we building this racetrack or not?' Grandma said, and opened the Infinite Race box with a *Drop it!* glare just for me. 'Look at this magnificent box! Who do you think drew it?'

'I don't know, but I think they made a Princess Elsa that's in the loft too,' I replied doubtfully.

The Infinite Race box was a *lot* ropier in the light. Whoever drew the pictures had spent all their time on their little squiggly lines, instead of learning how to draw. Most of the vehicles were all squashed on one side, like Celestine's birthday card messages, and the sizes were all wrong; a tiny tank trundling beneath a massive bicycle, a car about to run over a smaller lorry. Even Celestine looked disappointed, until she opened the box and lifted out the instruction sheet. On one side it said this:

Discover the Rules
Prepare for the Greatest Race of
Your Lives

'Ooooh, you see that, Celestine? *Discover the Rules*,' said Grandma. 'Shall we find out what they are?'

Celestine cheered up.

'*The Greatest Race of Your Lives*,' she said. 'They can't lie when they say that or it's False Advertising.'

I groaned. Celestine had learned about False Advertising recently, which meant she mentioned it about twelve times a day. But it looked like she was wrong this time, as we took out the pieces of track ... only to find that there were just *seven* of them.

'Seven pieces?' I objected. 'It's not very "Infinite", is it? How's that not False Advertising?' But Grandma dialled

25

up the warning look to Force 4 and I shut up to help assemble the track.

It was still hard not to moan. There might have been only seven pieces, but they didn't have any numbers or arrows on them to tell you which order they went in. Even worse, if you tried to connect the wrong ones they would SNAP together like a piranha's jaws, leaving the two pieces twisted and a nightmare to pull apart. By the time we had seven pieces connected, I'd lost the feeling in every finger, and the circuit wasn't even half complete, just a big curve with a chequerboard piece on both ends.

Worst of all? What I thought was a track, like Scalextric

or Hot Wheels, was just NOT. There wasn't a plug, wasn't anything to fire the cars along. There was just half a circuit, and nothing else.

'Check the box again,' Celestine said.

'What is there to check?!' I said, holding the empty box up for her to see.

'Let's have another look at those instructions,' said Grandma.

The Instructions were on the back of the sheet telling us to 'Discover the Rules', and they were the strangest I'd ever seen. Half the words had numbers instead of letters, and even the words I *could* read didn't make any sense:

THE INFINITE RACE

INSTRUCTIONS

STRING THE3RY-B8SED QUANTUM TRANSP3RTER

The Infin5te Race is fully compat5ble with all quantu1 theorie4 of space-t5me, super4ymmetry, and Schrödinger's 6at.

Features

- Full-w3rld liv5ng. B3dy displa9ement, 45ght, f9el, tas7e and t3uch.
- 3nly 4even pieces!!!
- Neg9ntropy.

4afety Notes

- Not su5table for 3bnoxious, rude or unpleasant 6h5ldren.
- FOR S3LID FORMS 3NLY! Attempts to en7er a l5quid f3r1 may 6ause naus9a.
- For all other Safety Gu5delines, please study Do6 67N2367N in *Quantum Mechanics Explained.*

4etting Up

1. Remove 8ll terb5um 7r8ck piece4 fr3m 7he bag.

2. Arrang9 the trac2 into a 'U' 4hape, so tha7 the ch9quered ends are the f5rst and la4t pi9ces.

3. On a 4quare of 45lk or rabb57 fur, D8NCE THE S7ATIC D8NC9.

4. Dr5ve the 6ar fro1 one end of the tr8ck to the other. The car 1ust b9 5n c3ntact with the 7rac2 at all times, fr3m the 4t8rt to the fin5sh.

5. Of c3urse, in a real c5r6uit, the st8rt *is* the finish.

6. C3ngr8tulations! You have play9d with 'Infinite Race'! If you 4eek 3nly a slap on the ba6k, 9njoy n3w, and g5ve it to 4omebody 9lse!

7. However, should y3u want the backsl8ps 7o be slapped ba6k, w3nder why you didn't start f8cing bac2wards, r9read steps 4 and 5 and !racecar rotavator ! rotavator racecar!

I mean, give me strength. Celestine leaned in to look at them too, and after a few seconds, she got up and walked out. I looked to Grandma.

'Do you think she's upset?'

'Who wants to play Nana Yaa?' Celestine said, coming back in wheeling in her stupid toy cookout set.

'*You're* the one who said we should make this stupid track!' I said, outraged.

'Yeah, but I thought it was *magic*. It's not done *anything*.'

'Shh!' Grandma said, engrossed in the Instructions. 'This is interesting.'

My heart sank. Grandma loves to tinker with things. Every Christmas she makes jewellery for presents, and when Mum's ancient MP3 player broke, she spent hours on it, even though Dad kept saying, 'You can't fix it. That's water damage, that.' (It still works. She tests it out in front of him every time she visits.) If Grandma was hooked, we were in it for the long haul.

'Look at the "features" bit,' she said:

Features

- Full-w3rld liv5ng. B3dy displa9ement, s5ght, f9el, tas7e and 7ouch.

- 3nly 4even pieces!!!
- Neg9ntropy.

'You know what feature I'd like?' I said. 'My fingers back.'

Grandma ignored me. 'What looks the same here?'

'Well,' I said. 'There's numbers where there should be letters. Whoever wrote this needs a new computer. Or tablet,' I added hopefully.

'Foolish child!' Grandma chided. 'What letters?'

'Well ... I think the first "feature" is supposed to say "Full-world living", but the "o" in "world" is spelled with a "3" instead of an "o". But then the second feature I think says "Only seven pieces", which, I don't know why they're bragging about that, but ...' I paused. *This is interesting*, I thought, despite myself. 'But the "o" in "only" is spelled with a "3" as well. And the "s" in "seven pieces",' I added, my fascination growing. '*That's* been spelled with a "4" instead, and *so* has the "S" in "Safety Notes", look. I *think* there's a "5" instead of an "i" in this bit, "living", and further down in "suitable" in the Safety Notes. It's, it's ... it's some kind of ...'

I looked up to Grandma, and palmed my fist. 'All the

31

"5"s are "i"s, all the "7"s are "t"s, and all the "3"s are "o"s! It's a code!'

Grandma's smiles don't come often, but when they do, they're pretty special. She clapped me on the back, and went out to the hall. When she returned, she had a notepad and a pen.

'Now let's figure out what the other numbers are and decipher these Setting Up instructions. Then we can race this Infinite Race, and Kyan can have two hours on his tablet.'

Celestine opened her mouth to protest.

'We're only allowed an hour on the—'

'*Two* hours he can have, because he didn't Give Up,' she said sharply, and Celestine looked guiltily at her cookout. 'And besides, I need to start the oxtail, the Formula One's on telly, and your mother and father aren't paying me to be here. OK, Ky?'

I didn't answer right away. I was too busy staring at the piece of racetrack I'd picked up.

Because without thinking I'd held it by the *Infinite Race* logo written along the side, the same fiery words that just that morning had come to life in the loft. The words were warm. And ever so slightly, they *glowed*. The weird events of that morning whirled through my mind, and for the first time I wondered: did they *actually* happen?

'All right, Grandma,' I said. 'Let's crack this code.'

4

Well, we did it. In half an hour, we cracked the code. Be honest. Does this make sense to you?

Code: $A = 8$ $S = 4$ $T = 7$ $K = 2$ $M = 1$ $E = 9$ $I = 5$
$O = 3$ $C = 6$

1. Remove all terbium track pieces from the bag.
2. Arrange the track into a 'U' shape, so that the chequered ends are the first and last pieces.
3. On a square of silk or rabbit fur, DANCE THE STATIC DANCE.

4. Drive the car from one end of the track to the other. The car must be in contact with the track at all times, from the start to finish.

5. Of course, in a real circuit, the start *is* the finish.

6. Congratulations! You have played with 'Infinite Race'! If you seek only a slap on the back, enjoy now, and give it to somebody else!

7. However, should you want the backslaps to be slapped back, wonder why you didn't start facing backwards, reread steps 4 and 5 and !racecar rotavator ! rotavator racecar!

Nope. Me neither.

'Who's got a square of rabbit fur, Grandma?' I moaned. 'What's the static dance? And terbium? Racecar rotavator? All this time I could've been playing on my—'

'Mention that tablet one more time, Kyan Green, and I'll throw it out the window,' Grandma threatened. 'That's the trouble with your generation – you don't know about feet and inches, you don't wash chicken properly, and you want everything done yesterday. Don't you know about the patient man and the donkey?'

'I could google it if I had my tablet,' I said sulkily.

'I know what terbium is,' Celestine said in a voice that oozed smugness. '*I* pay attention to your jewellery programmes, Grandma.'

'*You* would!' I said. 'If it's not horses on telly, it's tiaras and silly crowns. Nice of you to join us, by the—'

'What's terbium then, Celestine?' Grandma said.

'Terbium, is a type of, metal.'

'Oh, well, thanks—' I began, but Grandma cut me off *again*! Unbelievable!

'What about static, Celestine, do you know what static is?'

'Static,' Celestine continued, in a voice that somehow managed to be even smugger than before, 'is *electric*. It comes from balloons.'

'Excellent,' Grandma said before I could speak. 'Almost *perfect*, Celestine. Static electricity comes from making friction by rubbing some surfaces together. *Including*, as you said, balloons. Now, because you Took Part, and Didn't Moan, Celestine, you can test-drive the car.'

I was beginning to think Grandma was playing us both.

Celestine floated to the car box on a cloud of smugness. It's an old crisps box we painted, and slowly, carefully, she began to pick through all the random toy vehicles we have in there.

'Wait,' I said. 'There was a car that came with it! It dropped off the track earlier, and . . .' I looked out to the hall. I didn't know *where* it had rolled away to.

'It shouldn't matter,' Grandma said. 'Not if the Instructions work like they say they do. So long as it's metal, you can – *Are you finished picking yet, Celestine?*'

'I *think* I'll pick the F1 car first,' Celestine was saying. 'Then this Fairy Queen Carriage. Although the F1 car has a dent, so . . .'

Before she could finish, Grandma snatched the F1 car up.

'It'll do fine,' she said, 'and life is short. Now, put on your bobbly slippers.'

Celestine stared.

'What?'

'Your slippers, the penguin ones. Put them on, and do a dance. Like this.'

And that's when Grandma did the *strangest* thing. She got up, 'And . . . a one, two, three,' she said, and *danced*, up and down the room, rubbing her socks on the carpet, before clapping her hands, and saying, 'Ta-dah!'

'Dad's right, Grandma,' I said, gobsmacked. 'You *are* doolally.'

'Yeah? Hold out your hand then,' Grandma said. When I did, she reached out and touched it with her finger. There was a *snap!* and I felt a brief static shock.

'Oi!' I said.

'Name's Roy, not Oi,' Grandma said, 'and this is a clue about static electricity. Celestine has to make friction, place the metal car down on the track without letting it go, and that will make a circuit, and charge the track.'

'Huh.' That was, I had to admit, pretty cool. Celestine looked excited too, genuinely excited, and as Grandma started to dance around again, looking pleased with herself, she joined in, and the two of them did the electric slide across the carpet until Celestine burst out laughing, and fell to her knees, crouching excitedly over the track. She held out the racecar, lowered it to the racetrack, and at once we all took a deep breath . . .

And breathed out again, because literally nothing happened.

'Maybe you have to push it along to the end, eh?' Grandma said. So Celestine did: she pushed the car all the way along the track, pressing down harder and harder on the car until, as it reached the chequered strip at the other end of the curve, it gave the saddest little squeak I've ever heard . . .

And still nothing happened.

'I don't understand,' Grandma said. 'It didn't work.'

Weirdly, I felt a bit . . . guilty. Grandma had put all this effort into making *our* toy work, and Celestine had been *so* excited to see whatever it was she'd seen earlier. And what had I done? I'd just moaned. I'd just made fun. So what if Infinite Race turned out to be nothing more than a racetrack for toddlers, something where you pushed the car along mumbling '*Broom-broom-broom*'? Celestine looked gutted, and that just wasn't fair.

'Can I try?' I said. Celestine paused, to gauge if I was making fun, and then handed me the car. I got up, took a deep breath . . . and I Vossi-Bopped right across the floor, shaking my feet as I did, all the while thinking, *I am so glad my friends aren't seeing this*. Celestine stared, and Grandma clapped . . . and finally Celestine laughed and joined in. Soon we were all dancing around again, shocking the track, and, when that didn't work, shocking each other. Nothing happened, but Celestine looked happier again.

'Ah well,' Grandma sighed at last. 'I'm bushed. I had wondered about this last instruction, this "racecar rotavator", but . . . we'll try another day, eh?'

'Definitely,' both me and Celestine said, and we
exchanged a grin that said *I hope not*. I went to my tablet,
leaned over to pick it up ... and that was when things
went horribly wrong. Because there was a *zzipp!* and a
small blue spark went from my finger to the tablet.

'What?' I said. I pushed the power button, and nothing
happened. 'Uhhhh, Grandma?'

'What's that?' said Grandma.

'My tablet just sparked and now it's not switching on.'
I tried again. Again, nothing happened.

'Oh really?' Grandma sounded *interested*, which annoyed me. This wasn't *interesting*. This was life and death.

Grandma took the tablet from me and studied it.

'It's the static, I bet. You have to discharge it into something else before picking up the tablet, else it creates a short circuit. I should've told you.' Grandma has a way of saying sorry that is the least sorry I've heard anyone sound.

'Well, can you fix it?' I said, trying to keep my voice steady.

'Sorry, sweet'eart, I'm done with mechanicking for today!' laughed Grandma. My own grandma, and she was laughing, as if my life *hadn't* just crumbled. I saw Celestine start to play cookout behind her, smiling again, and my blood boiled.

I danced around to cheer her up – what's she doing? She hasn't even noticed. She doesn't care. She never even has to care.

'It's not fair!' I shouted. 'I could've played with my tablet, it was *tablet time*! Instead I was building that stupid racetrack for my stupid sister.'

Celestine looked up as if she'd been slapped.

'You're the one who broke the stupid tablet!' she said.

Before I could think up a retort, Grandma was pointing at me again.

'Kyan!' she said, shocked. 'Good young men don't talk like that about their—'

'I don't want to be good right now!' I shouted, waving my finger in her face. 'She's so selfish, why can't I be?!'

Like an old ninja, Grandma got up with startling speed. She leaned over me, face like thunder, and suddenly I understood why Mum said she was still scared of her.

'Apologise to your sister, young man, or you can go to your room,' she said in a low, deep voice.

'I can't,' I said defiantly. 'We're *already here*.'

True, that, but I regretted those words as soon as they came out of my mouth.

5

I. Was. Bored. Outside my bedroom, the first day of summer holidays was flying by; vanishing hours while my friends played football and had fun without me. Trapped inside my room, the day crawled to a stop, with old toys and a broken tablet.

So I read a story. Then I wrote a story – I have a notepad full of stories, a lot of which involve a terrible sister having to apologise to her hero brother – and I was just getting to the good bit when my eye caught the last step on that Infinite Race instruction manual, still lying on the floor:

7. However, should you want backslaps to be
   slapped back, wonder why you didn't start

facing backwards, reread steps 4 and 5,
and !racecar rotavator ! rotavator racecar!

It was strange. All the other steps made sense except that one. 'Backslaps to be slapped back'? What was that about? And that bit at the end was just bonkers; '!racecar rotavator! rotavator racecar!' What was with that punctuation – the exclamation marks at the beginning and the middle and the end, and . . . ?

'Hmph,' I said out loud. Because it wasn't just the exclamation marks that were at the beginning and end. Next to them, at both ends, was an 'r'. And next to *them*, at both ends, was an 'a'. It was like there was a mirror in the middle of the line:

!   !
!r   r!
!ra   ar!

I stared at the line in silence. Finally, I climbed down, picked up the Instructions and copied out that last bit. Only this time, I wrote it backwards:

!racecar rotavator ! rotavator racecar!

44

It was the same backwards as it was forwards.

'That has to be a clue,' I whispered. Step 7 also said to reread steps 4 and 5. So I did.

4. Drive the car from one end of the track to the other. The car must be in contact with the track at all times, from the start to finish.
5. Of course, in a real circuit, the start *is* the finish.

'So step four says to drive the car along the racetrack, don't let go,' I said to myself. 'Step *five* says that if it was a *proper* circuit, the start line would be the same as the finish line. And then step seven tells you to do something that's the same backwards as forwards.'

A light bulb came on in my mind.

I picked up the F1 car, and shuffled up and down the room, as quietly as I could. Next, I placed it back on the track, and pushed it to the finish line. Taking a deep breath, without taking my hand off the car, I pulled the car backwards. As soon as it was off the chequerboard piece, the track *clicked*, and I heard a woman yell through a very distant megaphone:

'Because KTG took the series lead from Spider Ace in the last race, she will be keen to snatch that back with—'

'Oh. My. Gosh,' I said, so surprised that I took my hand off the car. It made a little moan, like a posh trump, and the track *unclicked*, back to normal.

There was a knock at the door.

'Kyan?' said Grandma.

'Yes?' I said, trying *not* to sound like she'd interrupted the most earth-shattering moment of my entire life.

'If you apologise to your sister, you can come watch *Moana* on the memory stick.'

Well, you'll have to try harder than that, I thought. Grandma was always bringing her beloved memory stick, loaded with shaky films she'd got from her friends. Half the time the film ended right at the good bit, and even if it didn't, you had to listen to the other people in the cinema scoffing popcorn and slurping drinks. Besides, I was making groundbreaking discoveries here!

So I didn't answer, and after a moment, Grandma walked away.

I breathed a sigh of relief, and shuffled along the carpet again. Once I felt up to my eyeballs with static electricity, I held the car down on the track, pushed it to the end and pulled it back.

'We've got KTG's cannons, Xtina's cricket bat, Brigadier Borstal's Bashmonster, and of course—'

This was it. My finger trembled on the car as I looked closely at the track. All the joins between the pieces were gone. It wasn't even metal any more, it was a *real* road, a tiny, real, *tarmac* road, with even more potholes and scorch marks than our street. The car *revved* – my toy car, that just a moment ago had been as likely to rev as a banana – and I smelt that *burning* smell again, only more intense.

That's when a crowd began to roar.

'AAAAND, THEY'RE ALL VERY EXCITED TO BE HERE AT THIS GRRREAT MEMMMMMORIOUS OCCASION!' A woman's voice echoed around the room, and I knew what I had to do.

I had to race.

Heart in mouth, I pulled the car further back towards me and the engine roared into life with a *RRRRAAAR*! The chequerboard end lit up, the flaming letters *Infinite Race* crackled with a fierce heat. I felt a prickling sensation on my head, lifted one hand to touch, and felt my own curls standing on end, just as Celestine's had been.

She was right. This is big.

Out of nowhere, an impossible breeze lifted my clothes, making everything blur like I was looking through a cloud

of dust. But when I passed my free hand through it, I realised this *wasn't* dust. This was a cloud of *strings*, tiny, tiny strings, each one the colour of a rainbow. They were all coiling in the same squiggly shape, and as the cloud grew it became bigger and *bigger* until it wasn't a cloud, it was . . . everything.

And then 'everything' grew. Or I shrank.

First I noticed that the *car* was pulling *me*, not me pushing it any more. It no longer fitted between my thumb and forefinger either, but had stretched out like a Tonka truck. My high sleeper bed loomed higher, the size of a house, the carpet was a long, woolly wheatfield, and the track was . . .

'I'm . . . I'm crawling backwards along a *toy track*,' I gasped with an amazed laugh.

Then the car *sped up*.

'What?'

I tried to take my hand off and, with a yelp, couldn't. It was like the car's growing metal roof had some magnetic attraction to my hand! As the car revved, I shrank faster with it, until I staggered to my feet and back-pedalled frantically. Have you ever run the 100-metre sprint backwards in your socks? Well, I have *whooped* your record. Much more of this and I'd be a goner, but despite pulling with all of my strength, despite pushing both my feet against the car door, I still couldn't get free! As I reached the track's curve, as a deep and tangled forest of crumb-covered carpet hairs raced towards me before melting into billions of those squiggly strings, I let out a desperate cry, then did the only thing that made sense.

I jumped.

'OH MY—' the woman's voice reverberated through unseen speakers like a race announcer.

There was a sucking sound.

49

'OH MY MMMMMAGICAL MO—'

There was a tornado of wind around my ears.

'OH MY MMMMMAGICAL MOMENTS, WE ARE . . .'

I trumped. (Hey, I'm human.)

'OH MY MMMMMAGICAL MOMENTS, WE ARE GO GO GO!'

And I shot, feet first, into the front seat of the car. I'd done it! I was driving the car! But something felt wrong. The world around me began to take shape. I saw a sun, a sky, then buildings and trees, then a cheering, hollering crowd. The Infinite Race Instructions billowed over me, the size of a giant's bedsheet, and before the paper dissolved into nothingness, I saw those last words again and realised my mistake:

. . . why you didn't start facing backwards . . .

I was driving a racecar, on a real track, in a real race.

Backwards.

6

'We have KTG in the lead, Spider Ace following close behind! Behind *them* is the entire pack, except ... Kyan Green is ... He's driving ... HE'S DRIVING BACKWARDS! LOOK OUT!'

It was sunny, there were palm trees, and thousands of people were cheering my name. Oh, and I was hurtling backwards past them at the speed of a roller coaster, in a battered old racecar that I'd never driven before in my life.

'HELP!' I screamed. 'I'M NOT SUPPOSED TO BE HERE!'

I tried to look behind me, but there was *no* room in this car. I was strapped into what felt like a converted baby seat, and the harder I tried to move – left arm SLAM, right leg CRACK – the tighter this space became, with the cone-shaped windscreen in front of me making matters worse.

'HELP!! CAN ANYBODY – AAARGH!'

With a *whomp-whomp-whomp-whomp*, a pack of vehicles shot past me at lightning speed. They were every shape, size, and *weird*: three-wheeled cars, monster trucks and *an elderly woman armed with a cricket bat cackling on a dirt bike*. They flew past me and disappeared around the corner, more chaotic than a Year 1 football match.

'Help!' I screamed. 'I can't slow down!'

'Ky! Ky!' a familiar voice hissed at me. 'What in the Janet Kays are you doing?!'

Wait, that can't be—

'Grandma?!' I said. The voice came from a battered old walkie-talkie on the seat between my legs. I picked it up and pushed the button. 'Grandma, *help!*'

'*Grandma?!* Now's not the time to get sentimental with me, boy. It's Loretta when you're on the track, understand? Now press those brakes, you melon!'

'Loretta?' I said. '*Melon?!*' But my panic lessened, just a little bit. I realised my foot was pressed down hard on the accelerator, took it off, and pressed it down on the brake. Straight away I stopped, jolting forward against the harness, all the wind leaving my body at once.

52

'Now, pull the crudging paddle up!' Grandma/Loretta continued. 'Behind the steering wheel, like it always is!'

I found a lever sticking out behind the right side of the steering wheel, and pulled it up.

'Good. Now hold down the button on the dashboard.'

There was a small black button stuck to the dashboard with sticky tape. 'This one? What does that even do?'

'JUST HOLD IT DOWN, YOU MUSHY PLANK!' Almost-Grandma shouted. I pressed it down, and there was a *click-click-click-click*, like somebody was switching on a hob. She added: 'I told you I'd get that nitro boost, didn't I!'

'Nitro WHAT?!' I yelled, and just at that minute there was a *whomp!* above me. I looked up and saw a giant exhaust pipe gaffer taped – *gaffer taped!* – to the windscreen just as blue flames shot out of it, sending the car *rocketing* forward and pinning me back to my seat! My car veered off-road, beneath a red-and-white barrier, hurtling between drinks stands and Portaloos, before I TORE through another barrier, right back on to the track and right back between the other cars!

'GREEEEENIUS moves by the artful dodging Kyan Green,' the woman's voice boomed around me. We raced past a stand holding thousands of screaming fans, a huge screen opposite them. It showed my car – *my TOY car!* – careening across a side track on Instant Replay, before returning to show the commentator's mouth at the mic – although from down here I could only see her chin. 'He's rrrrrrright back in the soup and scaring the *heck* outta the pack!'

'I don't *want* soup!' I shouted. 'I just want to go home!'

Finally, my nitro boost wore off, everything stopped blurring, and I saw the other vehicles in this race. They weren't just racing. They were *fighting*, smashing into each other as hard as they could, throwing rocks, hammers and, in the case of the cackling woman on the dirt bike, swinging her cricket bat hard into anyone foolish enough to get too close.

'This looks dangerous, Gra— Loretta,' I stammered.

'Of course it's dangerous!' Grandma/Loretta snapped. 'That's why you've got the helmet on. Except . . . why isn't your headcam on my feed? DID YOU FORGET IT AGAIN?!'

Right in the middle of my dashboard, a flickering black-and-white screen came on, my grandma peering suspiciously in, nose first like she always does on videochat, only . . . only *this* Loretta's hair was longer, and straightened, whereas my grandma's is cut short . . . and *this* Loretta's face was a bit sharper where my grandma's face is a bit wider. This wasn't my grandma, I realised. It just . . . almost was.

'YOU'VE LEFT YOUR HELMET OFF, YOU SILLY BOY! AND WHERE'S YOUR RACESUIT?'

'I . . . I . . .' With my free hand I patted my trackies and T-shirt as though the helmet would somehow be in my pocket, so distracted that I didn't see the dirt bike slowing alongside me until I heard a cackle, and looked up to see some swaying jewellery, some thick-rimmed specs that I *swear* were carved out of bone, and two wild eyes, watching me with glee.

'Christine!' I squeaked. 'Shouldn't you be at church?'

'My name ain't Christine,' Almost-Christine screamed, pulling her bat back to swing. 'It's *Xtina*! Xtina Screamz, your biggest fan! Wanna sign my bat with your face?'

I let out a squeal – don't *think* that you wouldn't – and slammed on the brakes, only to hear the rumble of a massive engine thundering up behind me. It was the monsterest monster truck I'd ever seen, driven by a furious-looking man with a red face and one big bushy eyebrow in a straight line across his face. My back spoiler scraped and scratched against his massive grille, and even over the engines I heard him roar through a megaphone like a constipated troll.

'Fee-fi-fo-fum, I smell the oil of a KyanBUM!'

No way was I hanging around to find out what that meant. Luckily my car was faster than his truck. I slammed the accelerator pedal back down, shot forwards beneath Xtina's *swooshing* cricket bat, and heard it smash behind me into the monster truck's bonnet instead.

'YOU SCRATCHED MY PAINT!' the monster truck driver sobbed. I sped forwards, right between the two blue Minis about to ram each other, and as I glanced into my side mirror I saw them, the monster truck and my 'biggest fan' all colliding in an ear-splitting CRASH!

'Oh myyyyyyyyyyyyy tremulous tyre tracks!' the announcer's voice boomed out of megaphones, as a huge cloud of black smoke surrounded me. 'Exquisit*atious* driving by Kyan Green! He's taken out half the grid with just a few more to go! But is he hitting Dead Man's Curve too fast?'

As the smoke cleared I saw exactly what she meant. The road turned in a sharp bend to the left, and *kept* turning, until it turned all the way back in the other direction. It was a hairpin bend!

'Slow down, whiffbiscuit!' Almost-Grandma yelled through my radio. 'You've got no helmet! And remember what we said about taking hairpins? Outside – inside – outside.'

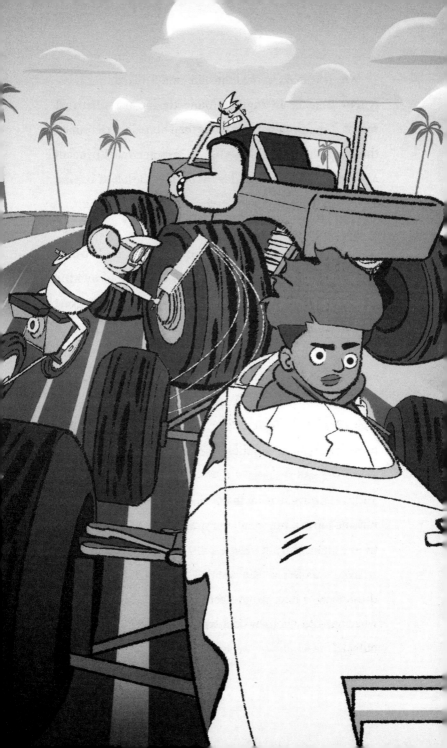

'Are you making these insults up?' I asked, but there was no time for an answer – Dead Man's Curve was here! I drifted to the right of the track, the *outside* of the curve, then just before it was too late, I slammed on the brakes and turned the steering wheel as hard to the left as I could. The engine whined. The tyres burned. *Make iiiiiittt!* I begged.

And I did! Just when it seemed like the wheels would spin off, the track straightened and I hit the gas with a 'WOOHOO!' And honestly? That was when everything *clicked*. You know when you just *know* you're good at something? A sport, or a game, or drawing, or distracting your mates in class? Well, without sounding like a bighead, that was me with racing. Two more corners came up, and I'd already figured out how to take them before Almost-Grandma shouted instructions through the radio at me.

I was nearly starting to enjoy myself, when I flew past a red soft-top car, its engine a noisy *HRRRRRRR*. It was driven by a woman with a jet-black quiff, a leather jacket and blue triangle sunglasses. She seemed proper chill, pouring a drink from a flask while steering with her knees – but as I screamed past her, she lifted a sawn-off shotgun and aimed it out of the window at my tyres.

'ARGH!' I shouted. 'PLEASE DON'T, PLEASE DON'T, PLEASE—'

That's when the strangest thing happened. The woman looked directly at me, and paused. We stared at one another for a moment, then, lowering the shotgun, she nodded her head and kept on driving, letting me roar ahead.

'Galloping gearsticks!' the announcer hyped. 'Kyyyyyyyan Green overtakes Spider Ace to SCREAM into second place. Do I have your entendimiento?!'

Second place? Shmecond shmace: shotguns were my limit. I wanted OUT. But then the announcer said something else.

'Aaaaaaand ... KTG passes the line to begin his FINAL lap, that's the FINAL lap for this maaaaagnificent Stringer Corporation's Smash'Em'Up Race *for a million pounds!*'

A million pounds. I'm racing for a million pounds.

Images flashed through my mind. Me with a new tablet. Me wearing shades like a rock star. Me buying our flat for Mum and Dad, them not stressed, not worried.

'Don't just scratch yourself, you mutton-chop mullet, USE THE LAST OF YOUR NITRO!' Almost-Grandma roared. And as I crossed the chequered line, I nodded, and pressed the button again.

'Winner, winner, chicken dinNNNNNNEERRNNNNGGGHHHHH!!'

Even though I was prepared for it this time, that nitro boost was blisteringly fast! Tears streamed out of my eyes, turns coming at me as fast as I could react, *sharp left – sharp right – right curve – left curve.*

'Look at Kyan Green *go!*' the announcer boomed. 'He's catching KTG!'

'*She* likes my driving anyway,' I said smugly as the boost wore off.

'Sima the Announcer?' Almost-Grandma said incredulously through my radio. 'Did you knock your helmetless head? I told you – don't trust her! She's paid by Ken The Git.'

'Ken the . . . Wait, KTG?'

''S what I said, isn't it? Today I even saw her hanging around the pits before the race began, taking notes on the drivers to give to him. I just hope she didn't see the loose bolts on our back wheel protectors.'

'Loose bolts on the *what*, sorry?' I squeaked, but before she could answer, a carnival of carnage thundered around the next bend towards me, followed by *that* cackle. Xtina Screamz was still in the race, nipping around a yellow, expensive-looking SUV as its driver tried to lap her. It was KTG, the driver I had to beat!

Trouble was, while everyone else here seemed to be driving bits of metal they'd dug out of a skip, KTG's car was *smart*. Its wheels were big, its body a beefy, shiny yellow, the words *KTG – Kenneth Tha GOAT* in black letters across the back. *The Greatest Of All Time*, I thought, and for the first time wondered if I even *could* win this race.

Still, Xtina wasn't fazed a bit. She sped her battered dirt bike around KTG, smacking his truck with her bat, then careering back behind him before he could barge her off the road.

61

'Ha-HA!' Almost-Grandma cackled. 'I knew she'd do us proud.'

'Xtina's on our side?!' I said. 'She threatened to sign her cricket bat with my face!'

'Well, you were driving rubbish, Ky,' Almost-Grandma replied. 'I never said I approved of her methods, but they work.'

Xtina darted back and forth, pinging the bat at KTG's side mirrors. As I pulled up alongside him, he lost his temper and screamed out of the window at her, the yellow-and-black visor on his helmet hiding everything but his spitting mouth.

'GET WITH THE PROGRAMME, YOU STUPID OLD WOMAN!'

KTG ducked back in as Xtina swung her bat hard into his bright yellow door, giggling uncontrollably. But he reached for a button on his dash, his lips pulling back into a nasty sneer.

'Xtina, look out!' I shouted, but it was too late. With a dread, metallic whirr, a sleek black laser cannon swivelled out from the back of KTG's SUV, blasting Xtina's bike through the air.

'No!' I shouted. KTG smirked unpleasantly, and man did I want to chase him, but as Xtina crumpled to the ground, I knew I couldn't leave her lying there. I screeched to a halt, and pulled up beside her.

'Xtina? Xtina, are you OK?' I said. 'Xtina?'

For a horrible moment there was nothing. I pulled at my stupid seatbelt, struggling to get out of the car, but I couldn't find the buckle. Then Xtina looked up.

'What you sitting around for?' she grunted, getting slowly to her feet. 'Listen to your grandma. Go whoop him.'

She didn't need to say it twice. I put pedal to the metal, screeching forward with a roar. The road twisted, left, right, right and left, zipping past faster and faster, until finally my hard work paid off. I turned a corner, saw Dead Man's Curve ahead, and there was that yellow SUV, not even a hundred metres in front. His laser cannon had swivelled back away.

'I don't think he's seen me, Loretta!' I said. 'What can I do? Where's my weapon?'

'Weapon?' Almost-Grandma snorted. 'There might be a bag of nails under your chair. We only had enough money for the nitro boost, and that's got to go back to the shop if we don't win.'

Some things haven't changed, I thought with a sigh, then shook my head.

63

'I'd better win then,' I said determinedly, and roared up behind KTG, trying to stay out of range of his blaster while hoping that those slipstream boosts in every racing game I'd played were real. Here's the crazy thing too: they were! My speed increased, pushing me right behind the SUV, and just as KTG slowed right down for the hairpin, I went for it, darting forwards for the lead . . .

And I would've made it if Sima the Announcer hadn't ruined everything.

'Kenneth Kenneth KENNETH!' she shouted through the microphone, her usual showy voice suddenly sharp. 'Kyan's just behind you!'

'Hey!' I shouted. Almost-Grandma had been right. What kind of announcer warned drivers about being overtaken? Immediately KTG's laser swivelled back out at me, blast after blast leaving smoking craters in the road as I veered left and right to stay in one piece. Still, I stuck close to KTG, close enough to see his startled reaction in the SUV's mirror, and halfway around Dead Man's Curve he launched across to smash me off the track.

'Y'got him, kid, teach that man a lesson,' Almost-Grandma said. Without pausing to think, I braked *hard*. KTG flew past my bonnet, and I floored the accelerator again as he went spinning into the dust, snapping my finger like a badman as I passed him.

'That's for Xtina, ya bully!' I said, and was about to roar to victory when, as if in slow motion, *another* laser cannon came whirring out from his front bonnet.

'NOOOOOO!'

Yes. And there was no doubt where KTG was aiming either. The laser pointed downwards, right at my back wheels. *Choon-choon-choon*, BLAST-BLAST!

Two shots was all it took. With the first shot I felt the clang of metal drop behind me, and I didn't have time to react before the second shot hit my back left tyre with a BANG!

Like a bomb had exploded beneath me, I *bounced*, a stream of sparks scraping horribly out from the left side of my car. My steering wheel spun wildly, throwing me right, then left. KTG sped up alongside me, and he was surely going to win. My dreams were dashed, I gave up all hope . . . and then I caught sight of the snide smile on his face.

'No,' I growled. The finish line zooming towards us both, I had one last crazy idea – my only chance. Reaching under my seat, I felt a small bag of nails and LAUNCHED them out of the window. They scattered out across the track, right beneath KTG's wheels, and *BOOOOOFFFF!*

His back tyre exploded like a grenade! Veering wildly, KTG tried to barge me out of the way one last time . . . and instead locked with my wheels.

'NO!' KTG cried. We hurtled towards the finish line, stuck together in a head-squeezing spin. My windscreen came loose and sailed off into the air. Drool and snot flew out of my mouth and nose, went right around my head and splashed my face – *eurgh!* – forcing my eyes shut as we whirled towards the finish line, with just one thought swirling around my head.

Letmewinletmewin letmewin letmewin let me win let me win . . . let . . . me . . .

Finally we stopped. I opened my eyes. We'd crossed the finish line, and the crowd was cheering. Had I won?

'And the winner iiiiis . . .' Sima the Announcer bellowed. I clenched my fists and begged my luck to help. There was a long pause, so long in fact that everyone started to get restless. I looked up at the big screen and briefly caught sight of Sima the Announcer before she turned away to somebody else in the booth.

'I *did* help . . .' she said, away from the microphone. 'It's not my fault he still couldn't—'

The screen cut to black. Everybody waited with bated

breath. Finally, Sima's voice came through the speakers. She didn't sound enthusiastic any more.

'And the winner iiiiiis . . . KTG. Kenneth The – uh – Goat wins the race.'

I groaned, seeing the gutted looks on the faces in the crowd reflecting my own, and I remembered my broken tablet.

I saw a huge bag marked £££ being lowered down from the stand, the sort of thing robbers take in cartoons, and I remembered football camp, my friends going when I couldn't.

I saw KTG hop out of his yellow SUV, arms in the air, bellowing to the crowd as he walked towards his prize money, and I remembered my parents' tired, worried faces. I remembered all of this in a nanosecond, rested my head back and closed my eyes. After a moment, Almost-Grandma spoke, her voice quiet.

'Kyan,' Almost-Grandma urged. 'There's no point hanging around. You get out of that car, and you graciously shake that mushy moshyhole's hand.'

'You can't say that!' I laughed, although I wasn't even sure it was rude. 'Anyway I can't. I can't even take my seat-belt off.'

'Can't even . . . ? When you get back here, we're getting

68

you checked out,' Almost-Grandma said. 'Just lift it over your head!'

'Over my . . .' With a growing horror, I lifted the harness that was looped around me and held it in one hand. 'Gra— Loretta, this hasn't been doing anything at all!'

'That's why you're supposed to wear a helmet!'

Suddenly I had to get out. I pulled at the door handle. It wouldn't open – *Just like our car at home*, I thought – and so I clambered through the smashed-open windscreen, out on to the bonnet . . . and was hit by a wave of cheers.

'KY-AN! KY-AN! KY-AN! KY-AN!'

I have to admit, it was good hearing that crowd shout my name. I stayed on the bonnet, and was just about to raise my arms in the air, or do a silly dance, or something that would've – let's face it – ruined the moment, when the cheers suddenly turned to boos.

'What did I do?' I said, but then I saw heads turning away from me to the huge screens dotted around the stadium. They were showing a replay, of myself and KTG locked together as we crossed the finish line . . . *and they showed my wheel crossing the chequerboard first!*

'CHEAT!' I heard a voice shout above the crowd: my Almost-Grandma's voice. 'CHEAT! Ky-Ky won fair and square. The man's a CHEAT!'

I saw him again then, Mr KTG. He'd nearly reached the bag of cash, his face reddening, and he was shouting into a microphone on his wrist.

'What do you mean, she's locked it? BREAK IN THERE AND CUT THE VIDEO! Sima? SIMA! SIMA, DON'T DO THIS, WE HAD AN AGREEMENT!' The boos built, and KTG turned to the crowd, waving up to them.

'Now, now!' he said with an uneasy laugh. 'There are always winners and losers in life, and—'

'CHEAT! CHEAT! CHEAT! CHEAT!' The chant broke out, cutting him off. KTG glared at me, and for a strange moment I . . . I almost recognised him. But before I could remember, that snide smile played with the corners of his mouth, the same look he'd given when he was about to blast Xtina off the track, and somehow I knew what was going to happen.

'He's going to run,' I said, and prepared to jump off the bonnet. 'He's gonna take the prize money and leg it! OYYYYYYYY . . .'

What a mistake. Because as soon as my feet left the bonnet, the world dissolved into strings again; the trees, the crowd, the sky above and even the tarmac beneath me. I fell through it into a bottomless hole, still 'Oy'-ing while strings and strange shapes shot past me like bullets from a gun.

'... YYYYYYYYYY ...'

For a nanosecond I was nowhere, surrounded by dark and luminous strings. Then the sound of an engine ROARED past me. It was the woman with the quiff and the blue sunglasses – *Spider Ace!* – the strings forming a road just ahead of her. She stared at me, a strange almost-smile on her face. Then I felt myself falling backwards, *still* 'Oy'-ing. The strings clumped together like Mum's spaghetti, strands, then lumps, then ...

'... YYYY—'

WHOOMPH! I landed flat on my bedroom carpet. Everything was back to its normal size. The toy car fell to the floor next to me with a clatter. The door opened, and a figure stood over me.

'My name's Roy, not Oi,' a voice said. It was my mum, and she wasn't laughing.

7

The whole street went quiet. Babies stopped crying, birds stopped chirping. Somewhere a cat began to miaow, then clasped a paw to its mouth. Finally, my mum spoke again.

'You've got some explaining to do.'

'All right, here goes. I've just used this racetrack to teleport *into* this toy car, right into the middle of a Grand Prix! I won the race, but this other driver cheated and *stole the prize!*'

. . . is what I *didn't* say. How could I? Mum would never believe me, I wasn't even sure *I* believed me! So I just stayed quiet.

Mum crouched down in front of me and sighed.

'You know what's most disappointing, Ky? Your dad asked for there to be no arguments this morning *especially*. And *you* ignored that and took all your anger about the tablet out on your sister.'

I didn't know what she meant at first. Then it hit me. *Mum doesn't know you've gone anywhere.* She must have just arrived back at the flat and been told I'd rowed with Celestine because my tablet was broken. That was it.

'Is Celestine still upset?' I said, picturing her wailing through the streets.

'No, she's watching *Rosalita's Riding School* with your grandma.'

'Oh.'

'So,' Mum said, 'after you've . . .' She paused and looked around. The track was back to normal, just seven pieces in a half-circuit. But everywhere else was chaos. The car box had been flung across the room with the Infinite Race box, the Instructions and about thirty toy cars.

'After you've tidied this mess,' Mum continued, 'you can apologise. *Properly*, not like, you know, *you*.'

'What does that mean?!'

Before Mum could answer, the doorbell rang and my Dad stomped downstairs to answer it.

'He's one of life's stompers,' Mum said fondly. But then Dad opened the door and her smile faded.

'Hi, Padraig, good to see you,' the bossy voice said. Mum got up and left the room.

It was Mr Stringer again.

By the time I'd finished tidying away the Infinite Race, I'd almost convinced myself that I'd had some kind of crazy dream, had somehow imagined an entire race. Almost, except . . .

Except it was so *real*! But what did that mean for me? Part of me wanted to take that racetrack to the nearest responsible adult and never touch it again. But a *bigger* part was still flush with adrenalin, was pacing the floor and ready to scream with excitement at what I'd just done. I was *this* close to unpacking it all again, when I looked up and saw Grandma watching me in the doorway.

'I'm going now,' she said. She was putting on her coat, looking at me with a little bit more warmth than earlier. I owed her an apology, I knew that.

But, *eesh* . . . There's something about that word . . . that S-word. I find it *sooo* difficult to say! Mum says I get it from Grandma, and Grandma says I get it from Mum, and

Dad says I get it from both of them. When I was finally able to look in her general direction, I said it.

'Sorry, Grandma.'

'OK,' she said with a slight smile. 'But it's not me you need to be apologising to.' She gestured to the front room, and I saw Celestine sitting in front of the telly, watching Rosalita get into yet another scrape, probably with some pesky bandits and with her friends Moxie and Annabella helping her. Urgh, I *hate* that show.

'Sorry, Celestine,' I said, and then looked back to Grandma. She looked disappointed. Everyone looks disappointed when I'm not perfect, and amused when my sister's naughty.

With a sigh, Grandma stepped away, and went down the stairs.

'Bye then, Celestine!' she called as she did. 'Thank you for a lovely day.'

'You're welcome!' Celestine shouted, not getting up, not even switching the telly off, like I have to when guests are leaving. Grandma laughed, and just before her head disappeared behind the banister, she looked at me once again.

'Have a think, Kyan,' she said with a meaningful gesture that would've been a whole lot more meaningful if she wasn't just a head. I nodded, really just wondering if she'd ever tell Celestine to 'have a think' if *she'd* been rude to *me*, when a thought occurred and I ran to the top of the stairs.

'Grandma,' I said. 'Did Auntie Christine ever ride a bike? Like a motorbike?'

'Christine from my church?' Grandma said with a grin. I started to grin myself, when suddenly her mouth dropped open.

'You know, it's funny you mention it. She always wanted a little tickover when we were sixteen, a little moped, but her father wouldn't hear of it. Probably for the best too – she had a pushbike before then and she was a terror on that thing! Some boys at school went for my brother once, and she chased them all the way home with his cricket bat!'

'OK . . . bye then, Grandma,' I said, stunned. Grandma shut the door behind her, and I stayed at the top of the stairs, trying to get my head around what I'd heard. Even if I'd just imagined the Infinite Race, what would *ever* have made me imagine Auntie Christine on a bike armed with a *cricket bat*?! So . . . did that mean I really *had* won a race somewhere? Did that mean I really *had* won that prize? As endless possibilities went through my mind, I heard Mr Stringer speaking snidely in the kitchen . . .

'I mean, get with the programme!'

And an even *crazier* connection occured to me.

I snuck to the kitchen door.

'Mr Stringer, be reasonable,' Dad was saying. 'I've said I'll fix the ceiling, like I keep fixing the roof, even though you've been promising to get someone in. Me and Cynth are working all the hours, and we've *never* been late for the rent. Please don't do this.'

'I'm sympathetic to your plight, Padraig,' I could hear Mr Stringer say smoothly, not sounding sympathetic at all, 'but I have a business to run. I gave you fair warning about the high demand in this area, and still you vandalised my ceiling, so your next rental payment *will* increase.'

'The *next* one?!' my mum said. 'That's ridiculous, that's Friday's rent! You can't do that!'

'I have to do that. As I said before, if you can't care for this flat and pay what it's worth as good tenants, then perhaps you should move to another area—'

'No!' I shouted. There was a dreadful pause, then I heard footsteps marching towards the kitchen door. Mum opened it but, worse than angry, she looked *upset*, upset that Mr Stringer was putting the rent up, upset that I'd heard it.

'Are we going to have to move?' I said in a quiet voice.

'. . . No,' Mum nearly whispered back. She turned to Dad, and they gave each other a small nod. 'No,' she said again to Mr Stringer, louder and firmer. 'This is our home. This is where we'll stay. We'll just find a way to pay it.'

'We'll see,' Mr Stringer said, looking down at me as if I'd just dropped out of a dog's bottom. 'There are always winners and losers in life. Now, if there's no other business to discuss, I'm supposed to tee off with some pretty important councillors *ten minutes ago*, so—'

'Actually,' I said, anger bubbling over into my *rudest* polite voice. 'Actually, can I ask one question please? How come you call my mum and dad by their first names when they call you Mr Stringer?'

Mr Stringer scowled. Mum looked shocked at first, then her eyebrows narrowed. She looked to my dad, and they both stood up a little bit straighter. After a moment, Dad nodded and walked past Mr Stringer to me, clasping a hand to my shoulder.

'Precisely, son. Now go apologise to Celestine and let us finish our meeting with *Kenneth* here.'

Kenneth. KTG. My crazy idea was right.

Mr Stringer was Kenneth Tha Goat.

I didn't apologise to Celestine. I went straight back to my room, but I didn't tidy up either. I had to think, to work out what was happening and what I should do.

I had journeyed through a toy racetrack into this *crazy* game, where people were *almost* like the people I knew here, and at the same time were *nothing* like the people I knew here. I'd won a race, but my prize money, enough to save our home from Mr Stringer, was stolen by the guy who *seemed* to be another version of . . . Mr Stringer.

My mind was literally twisted, and yet . . . I suddenly knew what I had to do. I had to race the Infinite Race again.

Not like before though. I needed help; not just help to win the race, but help to stop KTG from stealing the winnings. That meant people who wouldn't just run and tell on me (hello, Celestine), or who wouldn't just take the Infinite Race away (hello, every grown-up ever). I needed my friends. But without my tablet, there was only one way I could get hold of them.

'. . . I'll look forward to the payment on Friday,' Mr Stringer was saying as he walked down the stairs, Mum and Dad following behind him. As quickly as I could, I hurried out to the hallway and took my mum's phone from her coat pocket. With a few swipes and a password (my birthday, Celestine's birthday, obvs), I accessed my GroupMe and started to tap.

> PPL WYA?!?!?!?!?
>
> sumthing rubbish happened 🏠😨😱
>
> an sumthing 🔥🔥🔥
>
> got plans but need you guys at my flat tomorrow
>
> any way you can but low-key kpc 🤫🙈😶
>
> mebbe say it's last chance to see me b4 Football Factory 🏠✂️🐱

The cat emoji was a typo. Mum's phone has some weird emojis (which wouldn't matter if they'd get *me* a phone like *half of Year 5 already had*, hint-hint). But before I could tap a *correction, I felt somebody standing behind me. I looked up, saw Celestine, and froze.

'What are you doing?' she said, *infuriatingly* loud.

'Don't tell!' I whispered.

'Tell what?' Dad's voice came up the stairs.

Those dreaded words! Before I had time to put Mum's phone back he was at the top of the stairs. I stuffed the phone in my pocket and leaned casually against the wall.

Big mistake. Nobody leans on walls like that.

'What's going on?' Dad said. 'Nobody leans on walls like that. Did you say sorry to your sister?' His eyes went to my hands in my pockets, and his Spidey-senses tingled. 'What have you got there? Show me your—'

'He hasn't apologised yet,' Celestine said abruptly. Dad looked to her. 'I think that's why he's come out here.'

She helped me! I thought, and for a moment up was down, right was left. My sister *never* helps. Still, as boggled as my mind was, I had to play the advantage.

'You *always* suspect me, even when I'm doing nice things,' I said to Dad.

'Oh,' he said. 'Sorry.'

I turned to walk away, still shocked at Celestine's niceness, when she spoke again.

'Go on then. Apologise.'

There it was. I turned to see her smiling sweetly.

'Well?' Dad said, pausing.

'Sorry, Celestine,' I said through gritted teeth, and as Dad continued up the hallway,

a triumphant expression crossed her face.

'That's OK,' she said in her sweetest voice ever, before adding with a whisper, 'You can put Mum's phone back now.'

The world hadn't been turned upside down. Gravity wasn't pear-shaped. My sister hadn't helped me – she'd just found something on me. Now if I annoyed her, my whole plan would be ruined.

8

Both Mum and Dad had the whole morning off the next day. It was the first time in ages, and with my name in bad books, there was no way I could avoid the Green Family's Fifty-Mile Walk And Picnic™.

All right, I *usually* like it; we all help to make the picnic, which means this amazing spread featuring patties and chicken (made by me and Mum), plain ham sandwiches and a packet of some dutty Fisherman's Friend sweets (Tines and Dad, innit). But today? I just wanted to be getting back into the Infinite Race and winning it! It didn't help that my parents were clearly worried about Mr Stringer's increased rent, leaning in together with urgent whispers every chance they had, like I wouldn't twig what they were talking about.

Oh, and it *really* didn't help that Celestine had some-thing over me.

'Kyan!' she'd yell. 'Kyan! Look at this leaf!' I'd ignore her at first – if that sounds harsh, *you* try getting excited about the fiftieth leaf in a day. Then I'd catch a look on her face – that *I can destroy your life* look. Then, before I knew it, I was wasting *more* time looking at a speckly leaf. I was starting to despair of ever getting back to beat KTG and taking the prize money, when Mum's phone rang.

'Hi, Duncan,' she said, and my ears pricked up. Duncan is Luke's dad's name. Mum listened, and as she did, she glanced at me more, her face melting into one big smile.

'Awwwwww! That boy is just the sweetest!'

I had to hide my grin. Mum thinks Luke is an angel, and whatever reason he'd given to come round was *perfect*. 'Well, of course he can, he's never any trouble. This after-noon? He can stay for tea.'

After she hung up the phone, Mum was about to say something to me when it rang again. This time, when she read the name she looked suspicious. When I saw the name on her phone – Natasha Anev, Stefania and Dimitar's mum – I had a sinking feeling that I knew why.

'Heya, Natasha, how are you?' Mum said. She listened for a few seconds more, her eyes now piercing the

84

side of my head. 'Really? *And* Stefania said the same thing?'

I mean, Stef is supposed to be the clever one, I thought.

'This afternoon? Great, see you then!' She hung up the phone, and exchanged a look with my dad. 'It's funny,' she said. 'Luke, Stefania *and* Dimitar all had the same idea. Because they're worried that they'll miss Kyan at Football Factory, they want to come round today.'

Dad raised his eyebrows. I tried, and failed, to look as innocent as possible. And both he and Mum began to laugh.

'I didn't tell them to say the same thing!' I protested, but that only made them laugh more, until we were all cracking up. All except Celestine. In two phone calls, her iron grip on me was broken, and on the journey back home, she looked grumpy. Disappointed too.

'The Infinite Race! Yeah, so it's like ... like this crazy game, where you take your toy car in there and you get entered into a race for a *million pounds*. And I won the race! I'm a million-aire! At least I *should* be. But Mr Str— this other racer called Kenneth Tha Goat *cheated*, and *stole* my prize money . . .'

Celestine was at her friend's house, Mum was at work and Dad was somewhere fixing up the flat. So as soon as

Luke arrived, I explained to him my Plan, holding up a toy police car, and shuffling around the floor.

'Can you believe that?! So next time, I want all four of us to go in. If we're all playing, one of us *has* to win. And if KTG tries to make a run for it . . . I'll be in the police car to arrest him!' I finished triumphantly. It was a great plan, and I'd explained it perfectly.

But Luke just kept glancing between me and the police car.

'So . . .' he said slowly. 'You pushed that car along this track—'

'Not this car. The racecar.'

'You pushed this other car along this track, and it took you to another world. In the car.'

'Exactly.'

'And your grandma was there.'

'Not *my* grandma. My grandma from *there*.'

Luke blinked. He looked a bit tired.

'And it works with static electricity,' he said, looking at my shuffling feet.

'Yep.'

'Like . . . balloons on your head.'

'. . . Yep.'

'I don't see any balloons,' he said, and a bit of me cried inside.

'Luke . . .'

'What's the other rules?' he said, staring inside the box.

'. . . I don't know what you mean, mate, I—'

'The other rules,' he repeated. 'It says well done for completing your first mission but now we have to solve the next rule—'

I snatched the Instructions out of his hands. On the back, beneath the bit telling us to 'Prepare for the Greatest Ride of Your Lives', were more words than there had been before. Which was impossible.

Discover the Rules
Prepare for the Greatest Race of Your Lives

Congratulations on completing your first race!
You have levelled up to Level...

1

With your new Metamorphic Headphones, Level 1 Infinite Racers retain the clothing and communications enjoyed by their cosmic twins in every universe!

(Third-party devices also compatible. May be irreversible.)

'Metamorphic Headphones?!' I said excitedly. 'That's something *new*, Luke!' I looked in the box, and dug out . . .

'Er, I don't know if they're any different from regular headphones?' Luke said in his *nicest* voice, as I held up two sets of *very* old, *very* cheap wrap-around headphones, the kind that pull at least three strands of hair out when you take them off. 'Ooh . . . except somebody's cut the wire off, look.'

I put them on. Nothing happened. As my excitement faded fast, there was a knock at the door and my dad poked his head in, a blob of plaster quivering on the end of his nose.

'Stefania and Dimi's mum rang,' he said, and got that panicked look he has *every* time he has to remember one of my friends' parents' names. 'Mrs . . . Navel? Enrage? Enough?'

'Anev, Dad, Anev.'

'I said that! Anyway, they're running an hour late. Careful if you're coming out, I'm about to plaster.'

'With your nose?'

Dad gave me a funny look, then brushed his nose.

'Oh – ha! It's the Kiss FM *Countdown* an' all, so don't expect me to hear you if you want something or zombies invade.'

He shut the door, and after a moment began singing along to his tinny radio, voice too high, then too low. Excitedly I turned to Luke.

'My dad's working with his music on. We could set fireworks off in here and he wouldn't notice. It's the best time to Infinite Race!'

'What about Dimi and Stefania?'

I paused. True, my plan *had* involved them as well. But I'd beaten this Infinite Race game once without *any* help at all. Did I really need *three* teammates to beat it again?

'The timing's too good,' I said. 'Let's do this now.' But as I placed the car on the track, Luke held up a hand.

'Hang on.'

'What now?!'

'That police car looks old. Shouldn't we find something that, y'know, could win the race?'

'Well, of course, yeah, I . . .' I trailed off. 'Wait. You believe me?!'

Luke nodded, and for a moment I felt a burst of affection for 'me old mucker', as my dad likes to say. Soon we were looking through every police car I could find in the box.

'This one's got a massive exhaust, look!'

'Mmm, it's got no seatbelts though.'

'Yeah, but this one's got bigger lights, we could dazzle him!'

'Does it have seatbelts though, Luke? We *really* want seatbelts—'

'And look at the WHEELS on this – this would flatten the getaway car!'

At last we found a police car we both agreed on; the baddest-looking of the bunch, a beefed-up 4x4, with *PD* written down one side *and* seatbelts inside.

'That could take a hit from a cricket bat, three lasers and *still* chase Mr Stringer down when he tried to run off with the money,' I said with satisfaction.

'Mr who?' said Luke.

'Er . . . I mean KTG, the other driver. Kenneth Tha Goat.'

It was weird. I *wanted* to tell my friends about Mr Stringer and having to move, but . . .

But now their possible reactions went through my mind: Luke not getting why I didn't just *buy* a flat, Stefania saying something blunt like, 'You'll just have to move then.' Besides, we'd already picked out a toy police car, and Luke had put on the silly cut-off headphones. Telling him my mean old landlord was my nemesis in this race might just stretch even Luke's belief to breaking point. So without saying any more, I placed the police car on the track – backwards this time.

'Put your finger on the roof,' I said. Luke did so. And with a determined nod, I pushed the car to the end.

'Aren't we facing the wrong way?' Luke began, and I pulled the car back towards me. Like before, the track *clicked*, and a woman's voice came from far away, like Sima the Announcer's in the last race. Only – and this was *weird* – this time her accent sounded a bit *different*, and her voice came through all crackly, like it was coming through a walkie-talkie.

'Five-oh, five-oh, operation is a go-go—'

'Uh, Kyan,' said Luke. 'The track just talked.'

'I know,' I said excitedly. 'I am *so* glad I haven't lost my mind!'

The track was different from last time too. This road was rough, with potholes and cracks, with white lines through the middle like a normal road, not a racetrack. At the end, where there had been a chequerboard, was now a set of . . .

'Traffic lights?' I murmured. Something wasn't right here.

'Ten thirty-one in Crooklyn Heights, might cause a ten ninety then a ten eighty. Ten four?'

'Is it meant to do that?' said Luke. His face had gone very pale, his voice high and trembling, the way it goes when some kid challenges you to a fight you *know* you won't win. I tried to smile like this was all normal, but what was this about? Nobody mentioned Crooklyn Heights last time, did they?

'Five-oh, five-oh, robbery in progress on Starker and Wideroute, suspects may be armed and dangerous, so be careful out there—'

'Did she just say "armed and dangerous"?' Luke said, his voice even higher. 'Kyan, what's happening to the room?'

The car sped up, and we shrank, forcing us to drop to our knees and shuffle.

'As soon as you can, run,' I said. 'You need to run as *fast* as possible and—'

BANG! BANG-BANG-BANG! The sound of police sirens filled the room, an alarm blared, and somewhere glass smashed. The police car's wheels spun forwards, and the car shot *up*, all the way to my waist! I leaped up, but Luke sprawled over and was dragged along the growing track, a swallowing sound coming out of his mouth like a sea lion trying to beatbox, before he staggered to his feet and screamed, 'I – I CAN'T TAKE MY HAND OFF!'

'I said that would happen!' I shouted back.

'I DIDN'T BELIEVE YOU!'

'You didn't *believe* me?!'

'OF COURSE I DIDN'T BELIEVE YOU!' Luke tried to jump away, and slammed back into the side of the car, before struggling back to his feet again. 'IT'S A TOY FREAKIN' RACETRACK! WHAT IF YOUR DAD COMES IN?!'

'He'll just think we're playing hide-and-seek!'

'HIDE-AND-SEEK? IN THIS ROOM? WHERE WOULD YOU EVEN HIDE?! Kyan, WHERE IS YOUR ROOM GOING? WHERE IS YOUR ROOOOOOOOOO—?'

There was a sucking sound . . .

9

'FIVE-OH, FIVE-OH, WE ARE IN PURSUIT OF A STOLEN SQUAD CAR ACROSS CROOKLYN HEIGHTS, SUSPECTS IDENTIFIED AS THE BANK BLAG BOYS, THEY'RE ABOUT TO DRIVE RED LIGHTS ACROSS INTERSECTION THIRTY IN FRONT OF—'

'Lorries!' Luke screamed, and my vision cleared. I was sitting in the driver's seat of a police car with its siren blasting, and coming towards me were three lorries, too fast to stop.

Their deep horns blew, the earth shook beneath their rumbling wheels. But I'd done this before. I put my foot down and the car roared forwards, missing the last truck by a smidge.

'Ohhhhhhhh,' said Luke. 'Ohhhh. Oh, oh, oh, oh. Oh.'

'If you're "oh"-ing, you're breathing!' I said cheerfully, although part of me was wondering just where we had ended up. It was night, there were tall buildings, and bright lights, and traffic everywhere – traffic which got out of my way, thanks to the deafening siren and flashing light on top of our car. What there *wasn't* was racecars, or a cheering crowd. Clueless, I saw a burger van and slowed down to ask the man flipping burgers for directions.

'Excuse me, young man,' I said, trying to sound as old as possible. 'Do you know where the racetrack is?'

'IT'S YOU!' the man suddenly screamed. 'I DON'T WANT ANY TROUBLE! PLEASE!' And just like that, he sprinted down the street away from us.

'He must be a *criminal*,' Luke whispered. 'It's so *real*!'

I glanced at him. He was starting to smile now, at least, touching every part of the car he could reach. He wound the window down, stuck his head out, and pulled it back in, looking even more surprised with his hair sticking out every which way.

'Don't stick your head out, plonker. The lamp post'll knock it clean off!' I said, parroting my dad. 'Now, let's find a sign for this racetrack.' *It doesn't even look like the same*

95

country as before, I thought. *Where's all the palm trees? Where's the sea?!*

As my worries grew, a woman's voice came through the police radio on the dashboard. Straight away she sounded familiar, but . . . different too.

'All right, pay attention all units, this is Commanding Officer Sima,' she said, and my mouth dropped open. 'Stolen Squad Car Twelve is still at large, last seen crossing Intersection 31. We have choppers in the air and block-ades at the bridge, over.'

'Commanding Officer *Sima*?' I said. 'That's not Sima's voice! Though I bet those crooks regret stealing a police car.'

Right then, another police car burst out right behind us, its siren wailing as loud as ours. I couldn't make out the driver, though from the way he was waving his hands about I guessed he was pretty mad about something. Finally, he stuck his thumb out of the window and pointed it to the pavement. Not wanting to look like I didn't know what I was doing, I did the same, smiling extra wide to make it clear that this was just another day on the job. It didn't cheer him up though – he gripped a microphone pinned to his shoulder, and his voice exploded through the radio.

'Listen to me, Bank Blag buttheads,' he snarled. Again there was something familiar-but-different in the way he talked. 'Squad Car Twelve is *my* car, and if I think you're endangering lives in it, I WILL take you out, over.' He said it like it was something he hoped would happen.

'Flipping heck,' I said. 'I almost feel sorry for whoever stole that car! You best say something too, Luke.'

'What?! Why?' Luke said.

'Because everyone might think we look too young to be real police officers! Tell them . . . tell them we're hot on his heels.'

'Where's the walkie-talkie?'

'Somewhere on the dashboard, mate, just . . .' But Luke was right, there was nothing there. We looked all around the car, before Luke felt something on his chest. Looking at me, impressed, he pulled out a cable. On the end of it was a walkie-talkie just like the angry officer had.

'*Metamorphic Headphones*,' he whispered. 'The Instructions said we'd "retain the clothing and commun-ications" in every game, Kyan, look!' With that, he put the earpiece in, and gave it his best shot.

'Erm . . . can you hear me? Because *we're* police officers!' He gave me an important nod, and added, 'We are hot in his heels, over?'

'That . . .' I said, 'that was perfect.' (Sometimes it's nice just to be nice.)

'I don't think I could take anybody "out" though,' said Luke nervously.

'Don't worry,' I said. 'As soon as we find the racetrack we'll leave them. We don't want to push our luck. We're a couple of kids. We're not even wearing police uniforms!'

'What *are* we wearing?' Luke said. Somehow in the journey here our clothes had changed. Luke was wearing what looked like an undertaker's suit, which *kinda* just made him look like a ventriloquist's dummy. Meanwhile, I was all in black; black trousers, black gloves, a black jumper and even a black balaclava rolled down around my neck.

'Hmm,' I said. 'Maybe those Metamorphic Headphones are a bit faulty. They did look old. I don't even know if I've got a walkie-talkie.'

I *did* feel something soft digging into my back though, and pulled it out. It was two rubber cartoon masks, that *almost* looked like Donald Duck and Mickey Mouse.

'Heh, Luke! Look at these masks! We aren't very tough coppers!' But Luke had craned around to look at the back seat. When he turned back, his eyes were wide.

'Kyan!' he shouted. 'We might not even need to find the

racetrack! I think I've found your money!' As he pointed at a huge stash of banknotes piled up on the back seat, the angry policeman's voice exploded through the radio once again.

'I'M COMING FOR YOU, DIRTBAGS. OFFICER STRINGER IS COMING FOR YOU!'

'Luke,' I said, my throat dry. 'I *do* know that voice. That's Mr— That's KTG, Kenneth Tha Goat! The one who stole my prize money!'

Luke looked at me in surprise.

'Kenneth Tha Goat's a policeman as *well* as a racing driver?!'

'No!' I said. 'It's . . .' Something was beginning to make a dreadful sense. 'It's *another* KTG.'

I looked down at the dashboard. On it was the number 12.

'Luke,' I said. 'I don't think that's my money.'

Four more police cars screeched out behind us, their sirens clashing like angry beasts.

'Luke,' I said. 'I don't think this is the same place as last time.'

Swooshing in above us was the *pita-pita-pita* of a helicopter. I looked up to see a blinding light, shining down at us from the sky.

'Luke,' I said. 'I think they're chasing *us*!'

10

'I hope you're ready, Smith and Green! I'm taking you *down*!'

With flashing sirens and the *grrrrrOWL* of a powerful engine, Mr Stringer aka Kenneth Tha Goat aka Officer Stringer of Squad Car Thirteen smashed full-on into the back of our SUV, and sent us swerving violently across the road.

'Just my luck,' I moaned, speeding and straightening up. 'I try to be a cop, and turn into a robber instead!'

Luke didn't answer, but he pushed the TALK button on his earpiece and shouted into it.

'Your honour!'

'Your honour?!'

'Your honour, this is Luke! We didn't mean to take the police car! Or rob a bank! Please let us pull over so you can take it home!'

'Too late, Smith and Green,' Officer Stringer snarled through the radio. 'It's time you learned not to come to *my* streets and steal *my* squad car.'

'He knows our names . . .' Luke said faintly, 'how does he know our NAMES?' – as Officer Stringer *smashed* into the side of our car, snatching out through his window to grab for Luke.

'No you DON'T!' I retorted, and veered away. I was just thinking *Nice driving, Kyan!* when I saw Luke's terrified face. Guilt noogied at my skull. I hadn't meant for this to be a horrible experience, but he was *hating* this. *Another* squad car pulled out alongside us and he ducked back with a shriek. Thankfully this officer wasn't as shouty as Officer Stringer, and even though her face was mostly hidden by large sunglasses and a police cap, I recognised her as soon as she began to speak.

'Urban decay?' Officer Sima said, and pointed a thumb at herself with a cool-beans grin. 'It's time to meet the toothpaste. I knew we'd get you kids in the end. Pull over, Smith and Green, and let's hand back the bank's ill-gotten gains, shall we? I don't think you guys wanna see anybody hurt.'

'Forget that, Sima!' Officer Stringer sneered. 'I'm getting this criminal scum off my streets for good.' His engine roared, and he barged between us and Officer Sima, forcing her to one side with an angry yell and pushing us on to the kerb.

'What in the mother of . . . ? *Thirteen, suspect is surrendering, fall back NOW!*' Officer Sima shouted, but I didn't wait to see if Stringer would listen. I slammed on the brakes, pulled the wheel hard right, and drifted down a side road, breathing out, the most confident I'd been since getting here. There was no avoiding it, the chase was on.

And Stringer *still* wasn't as good a driver as me. As I darted in and out of traffic, his car barrelled straight down the middle of the road, forcing the other cars to swerve out of the way with their horns blaring. These bullying tactics made him faster than me, but each time the menacing guard grille on the front of his 4x4 threatened to smash into us, I would screech around the next turn, leaving him floundering behind us with a roar of rage. Yet still, no matter how far away I'd get from him, he would seem to pull out behind us just another street away.

'I don't get it!' I gasped, wrenching the roadster's wheels out of a drift on to a skyscraper-lined road, only for Officer Stringer to cannon out behind us just one street back. 'How's he keeping so close?'

'The siren!' Luke yelled. 'He's following the sound! We need to switch it off!'

We must've pressed every button we could see. After turning up the heating, blasting out the radio, and putting the wipers on so fast I thought they'd fly off, the siren was still blaring. Left turn, right turn, left, left, right – and *still* Thirteen was on our tail, bullying, threatening, endangering every other car on the road.

'Kyan,' Luke said.

'Just a sec,' I muttered, swerving yet another corner.

'*Kyan*,' Luke repeated.

'I can do this . . .'

'*KYAN!*' Luke insisted, and though his voice trembled, his face was set. 'If we keep running away, this guy's going to hurt someone. We should hand ourselves in to Officer Sima.'

I sighed, bitterly disappointed. Twice now, my chance of winning big at this game had been ruined.

'I guess you're right,' I said. 'But how do we give ourselves up without Officer Stringer running us off the road?'

'OK then, ALL UNITS!' Officer Sima's voice crackled through the radio, as if she knew what we were thinking. 'The bridge is being raised and every exit is blocked. Report to the bridge, *all of you who want this over peacefully.*'

'*All of you who* . . . ? I think she means us, Ky,' Luke said. 'That's our way to safety!'

I screeched around another corner and saw it in the rear-view mirror: a cable bridge at the end of the road, lifting up like a drawbridge into the air. Police cars were pouring out from every side street, forming two lines of flashing red and blue lights that led up to it. I slowed down, ready to turn and follow them . . .

And then *another* squad car screeched out, two roads ahead. For a moment it drove slowly, as if the driver were looking for someone. Then it *burned rubber*, barging across the road as it accelerated *straight for us*. It was Officer Stringer, and right then I knew for sure that he would do *anything* to take us out before we gave ourselves up peacefully.

The only way, I thought desperately, *the only way is if he doesn't know which car we are.*

'Ky? Ky, it's Officer Stringer!' Luke said. Stringer barged between two other squad cars, forcing them off the road as he sped up, close enough now for me to see the twisted, *hungry* smirk on his face.

'OK,' I said. 'You're right. Let's hand ourselves in.'

'That's good to hear, Ky, but he's going to wipe us ou—'

'Good job there's seatbelts,' I said, and put my foot down. Our car *raced* ahead, straight for Officer Stringer!

'Kyan!' Luke shouted. 'KYAAAAAN!' There wasn't a millisecond to explain. With Officer Stringer's headlights flooding my vision, at the last minute I veered right, swerving past him close enough to hear his bellow of rage and see him spin his steering wheel in a desperate attempt to turn around for another shot at us.

'Phew!' Luke began. 'I thought we were ...' But the second we were past Stringer, I pulled up the handbrake and *wrenched* the wheel all the way around.

'Aaaaaaaaaaaaaaaaaaaaaaaaaaaaaaaaaaaaaaaaaaaaaaaargh!' Luke yelled, as we screeched a doughnut right around Squad Car Thirteen. Completely bamboozled, Officer Stringer turned left, then right – and veered SMACK into a lamp post. The moment we were facing back towards the rising cable bridge and the other police cars, I pulled out of the spin, changed down gears and slammed the throttle, racing between and ahead of as many of the other police cars as I could. Finally sure I was far enough ahead, I eased off the pedal, eased on the brakes ...

... and slotted gracefully into a gap between the police cars. By the time Thirteen had turned around, our car looked like every other police car on the street, and we were like every other police officer. Well, almost.

'*Luke,*' I murmured through tight lips. '*Take Donald and Mickey off the dash!*' Luke knocked the masks down with trembling hands. For a moment we didn't dare move. Car Thirteen rolled past, his sneering voice passing by the open window as well as through the radio.

'Dispatch this is Thirteen, I've lost the perps. I strongly advise that you tell me where they are, over ...'

Finally, Stringer's voice faded away. Luke turned to me. He was smiling.

'We did it,' he said, starting to laugh. 'We did it! We did it, we did it! Now let's give ourselves up to Officer Sima and *go home*.'

I laughed, and was about to agree with him, when I caught a proper glimpse at the pile of banknotes in my rear-view mirror.

Oh my gosh, but it was so much money! *Enough to keep our home*, I thought, and another idea popped into my head. The bridge was still rising slowly at the end of the road. There was a gap between the two lines of police cars. It was big enough to fit through.

'Kyan?' said Luke.

The reason everyone likes Luke isn't because he's polite. It's because he's *good*. Bad actions are his kryptonite. Now, my Grand Prix prize money? That was mine, fair and square. The pile of banknotes sitting in the back of this stolen police truck? That was *nicked*, and just because *we* didn't nick it, didn't mean that Luke would be OK with me keeping it.

But I really didn't want to move away.

'It's just a game, Ky,' I whispered to myself. 'Nothing here counts *really*, does it?' The trouble was, part of me was already figuring out that this wasn't true.

'Twelve?' Officer Sima asked. 'Are you ready to get out of the car?'

'She's asking if we're ready to get out of the car,' whispered Luke.

'Twelve, I can see you.'

'She can see us, Kyan!'

'Sorry, Luke,' I said. 'Sorry, Commander Sima. I have to do this.' And I pushed down the accelerator, pulling forwards and to the left, between the two lines of police cars.

'Smith and Green, don't be foolish,' Commander Sima warned. Guessing what we were doing, the other police officers drove closer towards each other, tightening the gap until our wing mirrors smashed on both sides.

'Kyan, no!' Luke screamed.

'We can make it,' I said. 'We can jump the bridge!'

I put my foot down, and with a final roar, we burst clear of the police cars. Just when I thought we were clear, I saw Car Thirteen roar at me from the right, its mean-looking grille aimed straight for my door, saw Officer Stringer smile behind big, dark sunglasses.

And that was when I saw *another* Grandma. Her hair was up high, she wore a tracksuit and matching cap which

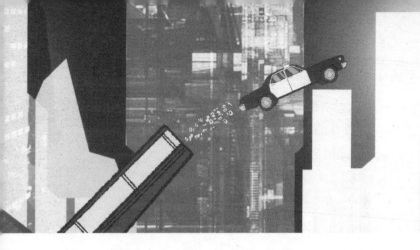

my grandma would *never* wear, and her accent was as different as Sima and Stringer's had been, but she still had the same love in her eyes as she ran towards me *straight* in front of Officer Stringer's car.

'Don't hurt my Ky-Bear!' she shouted. But Officer Stringer didn't slow down – he accelerated!

'Grandma!' I screamed. But just before she was hit, another police truck smashed into Squad Car Thirteen, pushing it out of the way at the last minute.

'No deal, Thirteen,' Officer Sima said. Unharmed, I sailed past her, the whole world silent and slo-mo, desperate disappointment in Sima's and my Almost-Grandma's eyes. I tried to mouth an apology, an explanation, but pushed my foot down instead.

That was when I realised Luke wasn't sitting next to me any more. He was in the back seat, opening the door.

'Luke, what are you doing?' I said. But his face was wild.

'This money ISN'T OURS!' he shouted, and before I could stop him, he lifted both feet, and kicked into the pile of banknotes.

'Luke, NO!' I screamed, but it was too late. Most of the money fell, tumbling out of the car in one fell swoop. With one hand on the wheel I snatched back, battling to save the remaining notes before he could push them all out. We struggled for one moment, as the truck's tyres left tarmac and we *soared* over the gap in the rising bridge. But Luke wouldn't stop. He shoved my hand away, *hefted* the last of the notes out . . . and overreached. With a look of growing horror on his face, he flew backwards and . . . fell out of the car.

'Luke!' I yelled. I shoved open my door and leaped out after him.

The wind blew.

Gravity pulled.

And the universe dissolved into strings.

'Luke!' I yelled again, flipping around like a fidget spinner. I saw him tumbling in front of me, banknotes fluttering around us like leaves, reached out to grab him, was *nearly there*, but then . . .

Out of nowhere there came the *HRRRRRR* of another engine hurtling past me, sending me spinning back with enough G-force to close my eyes. By the time they'd opened again, Luke was gone and the strings were merging into . . .

WHOOMPH! My back hit my bedroom carpet, and for a moment I lay there, the wind knocked out of me. I opened my clenched fist, and saw nothing inside. The money, even the last clump of notes I'd grabbed, all of it was gone. But right then, that didn't matter a bit. I stood up slowly, frozen with disbelief, when the door swung open. It was Dimi and Stefania.

'Ce faci, homes?' Dimi said, smiling, but Stefania cut him off, sniffing the air.

'This room stinks,' she said. 'And you look like you want to cry. What happened? Where's Luke?'

That was the real problem. Luke was nowhere to be seen.

11

'Hold up, hold up. Stuck in a toy car?' Dimi said, a disbelieving grin on his face. 'I didn't know you guys still played with them!'

I bit back an angry response, and glanced to Stefania in the hope that she'd look up from reading the Instructions. Dimi's safe, but he's also . . . well, *safe*. He's into sports, and music, and music and sports apps on his phone. Journeys to other worlds? That's not the kinda thing he'd imagine, let alone believe in.

I saw the toy police car, lying roof down on the floor, and a horrible, desperate hope occurred to me. Scrambling to the rug to pick it up, I gazed inside to see if a little toy Luke was rattling around inside it. But there was nothing.

'So what you're saying is,' Dimi continued, walking towards the racetrack, 'if I take this little fire engine, and drop it on the track just like this, I'll get . . . La naiba!'

'You DON'T need to make fun . . .' I turned to snap at him, and then I paused. Dimi's eyes were bug-like with shock. He knelt down by the track, and I saw what had surprised him.

'Oh my days,' Stefania said.

The track was missing.

Well, not *missing*. There was a track-shape there where it had been before. But it was a track-shape of *nothing*,

completely black, like someone had cut it out on a photo editor and forgotten to paste it back. The toy fire truck Dimi had been holding just a moment before was floating gently in the air above it. Dimi reached out to touch it, and . . .

'Stop!' Stefania shouted. Dimi froze, hand outstretched. Stefania shoved the Instructions into my chest. 'What have you done, Kyan? Where did you take Luke? Did you even read the Instructions properly beforehand? Did you even read the *rules*?!'

'Yes!' I said defensively. 'OK, well, not all of them. I . . . I just thought this was a game, this *epic* racing game, which I *should've won*, and . . . Stef, I don't think that game is just one level! And that last level was *huge!*'

'No kidding,' Stefania snapped. 'This isn't a game! It's called a *String Theory Quantum Transporter*! And if *this* thing's right, you've lost Luke in *another universe*, Kyan!' She shoved the Instructions into my hands like she'd rather smack it over my head. The words had changed again.

Prepare for the Ride of Your Lives

Congratulations on completing your second mission! You have levelled up to Level...

2

Level 2 Infinity Racers get to hop across the multiverse, all while understanding the rules that help prevent their brains from being disintegrated!

The Rules of Hopping

1. Only one version of a Hopper can be present in a universe at any one time. When you enter a universe, your cosmic twin is 'bumped' – suspended in the strings outside the universe until you have left – so that you can play as them for as long as you want.

2. A Hopper can only remain in the universe they're playing while they are held there by their mode of transport. Once you're out, you're out.

3. To join another Hopper in a universe already being played, you must find a vehicle which fits.

I stared at the list of rules, my mind well and truly blown.

'*Prevent their brains from being disintegrated?*' I said. 'I thought this was safe! What kind of nutter only gives you the rules to a game that risks brain disintegration *after* you've already played it?!'

'What kind of nutter doesn't think to check?' Stef said icily.

'That's . . .' I began to admit. 'That's an interesting way of looking at it.'

'This is *blatantly* a joke,' said Dimi. 'You're playing foolish, innit, Ky?' But he looked a bit less sure now. The fire engine floated past his head, and he batted at it frantically like it was a wasp. A horrible lurch of guilt rose, from my belly to my throat.

'I've got to go back in,' I said. 'I've got to go and get Luke.' I picked a toy Ferrari up off the floor, and stepped towards the track . . .

'Kyan!' Stef shouted. I paused, and looked at her.

'We *have* to figure this out properly. Before you go.'

'Why?' I said angrily. 'Give me one good reason why I don't just take that Ferrari on to that track and use it to save my friend.'

'Because. Ferraris. Don't. Go. Into. Space.'

I stared at the track in shock. It wasn't *just* black nothing. Really faint little stars were dotted around, like tiny pins. And hanging behind the fire engine, frozen in mid-air, was a small toy spaceship.

'Are you sure Luke is stuck in a car, fam?' Dimi asked quietly. 'Not a spaceship?'

'Oh my gosh,' I murmured. 'What do we do?'

'First? We're going to figure out just what this Infinite Race is,' Stefania said firmly. 'And *you're* going to explain to us what those rules mean.'

'OK,' Stefania said, reading through her phone. 'OK. I've kind of got a handle on String Theory now. How about you guys?'

I stared blankly back at her. In front of me were the Instructions, a copy of *Fun Science Facts* and my notepad on which I'd written four words:

Infinite Race — What is?

'Dim?' Stef asked.

'Eh?' Dimi said, lifting one headphone. It was playing music, and I don't think the music had anything to do with science. Stefania's nostrils flared, and she batted his 'phones off his head.

'OK,' she said. 'Listen up.'

'String Theory thinks that everything in the universe – me, you, this flat – is made of tiny strings. These tiny strings vibrate in their own special way. Almost like they play a note, like on the piano. *LAH!*' she sang, suddenly, and I flinched. Singing is *not* her A-game. 'Now, imagine this *LAH!* was the only note you had ever heard. Guitars, pianos, triangles – imagine that's the only note they play. *LAH! LAH! LAH!* You try it.'

'. . . Lah?'

'Nice. Now, if you played this *LAH!* on every instrument ever made, and you'd never heard any other notes, you *might* think it's the only sound there was, right? The instruments might *sound* different, but actually, in one major way, they're all the same. That's what String Theory says about all of *us*. Everything in this world, everything in this universe, me, you, tables, trees, galaxies . . . they might seem to us like completely different things, all different, but in *fact*, it's all coming from the same note. We're *LAH!* from a guitar, this bed is *LAH!* from a piano, the trees are *LAH!* from a guitar AND a piano. Right?'

'I've got *no* clue what you're saying right now,' said Dimi.

'*This racetrack plays the other notes*,' Stefania said urgently.

'So . . .' I stared at the track. 'This racetrack takes us to other universes *like* ours, but they might be slightly or majorly different.'

'Exactly,' Stefania said with a satisfied nod. 'It's the multiverse. Our universe, repeated again and again, billions and trillions of times.'

'Well, I get *that*,' Dimi moaned. '*That's* in every comic book film ever! How does that help us find Luke?'

'I . . .' Stefania said, and her shoulders slumped. 'I don't know.'

Then something caught my eye.

'I do,' I said, and shoved the box lid to them. 'Look at the Third Rule of Hopping.'

3. To join another Hopper in a universe already being played, you must find a vehicle which fits.

'The *track* looks at the *vehicle*, and figures out *what note to play*! The universe you end up in depends on the vehicle you choose!' I said excitedly. 'To find Luke, we'll need to be in a spaceship! And . . . Wait!'

I hurried to the track, and got as close as I could to the toy spaceship hovering in mid-air. It was a tiny ship, and it

121

didn't seem familiar at first . . . until I recognised the tiny plastic prongs in each side. *Like it docks with something else*, I thought, and lay flat on the floor so I could make out the logo stamped across the bottom of it.

'*Europa Scout*,' I read. 'This isn't just a single spaceship. This is part of a set! My mum got them at a car boot *ages* ago, when she was trying to get Celestine off princesses, only . . . *Tines never played with it.* It's been in a box all this time with . . .'

I ran to the toy car box and rummaged around.

'Here!' I shouted, taking out the box. '*Europa Quest – Now with Europa Quest Scout Ship Attached.* And wait . . .'

The box was already open. I slid out the clear plastic container inside, and lifted out the *Europa Quest*. It was a grey, basic-looking toy spaceship with an empty docking station in the middle.

'Luke's in the scout ship!' I exclaimed.

'Good,' Stefania said. 'What about the first two rules? Do they tell us anything important?'

The Rules of Hopping

1. Only one version of a Hopper can be present in a universe at any one time. When you enter a universe, your cosmic twin is

122

2. 'bumped' – suspended in the strings outside
   the universe until you have left – so that you
   can play as them for as long as you want.
2. A Hopper can only remain in the universe
   they're playing while they are held there
   by their mode of transport. Once you're
   out, you're out.

'The Second Rule's easy,' Dimi said. 'It must mean . . . to leave the universe, you have to jump out of the car, or ship, or whatever. Yeah?'

'Yes!' I said. 'Huh, that makes sense. When I jumped out at the racetrack, I left the racetrack universe, and the same when me and Luke fell out over the bridge!'

'Great, and . . .' Stef paused, and looked at me. 'Wait, are you saying you jumped out of a moving car *without* knowing it would take you home, or are you saying you went into that track without knowing how to get back out again?'

'Uh . . . both.'

'Give me strength,' she muttered. 'What about Rule One? What does that mean?'

1. Only one version of a Hopper can be
   present in a universe at any one time.

> When you enter a universe, your cosmic
> twin is 'bumped' – suspended in the strings
> outside the universe until you have left –
> so that you can play as them for as long
> as you want.

'. . . Right, well, that one I don't get,' I admitted. 'Unless . . .'

'Unless what?' Stef pressed.

'Well . . . When I was in the last universe, the other pol— uh, racers,' I corrected hastily (given Stef's reaction to the whole car-jumping-out-of thing, I *really* didn't see the need to get into the whole police-chase-and-stolen-money thing), 'the other racers all *knew* me, or at least *about* me. And in the first race, I was speaking to my grandma, only it wasn't my grandma, it . . . almost was. Like I wasn't just visiting there, but I had my own life. Like I was a completely *other* Kyan.'

Like another Kyan, who you left tumbling from that car, a small, nasty thought said at the back of my mind. I tried to push it aside – there was enough to be worrying about right now – but what *had* happened to the other Kyan and Luke, the Bank Blag Boys we left in that other universe?

'I still don't get it,' Dimi was saying. 'What do you mean, *other* Kyan? *You're* Kyan.'

'It was a *DAH* Kyan,' I said. 'In *DAH* universe.'

'What universe?!' said Dimi. 'The Da Universe like The Yes Universe, or Da Universe like Da Universe?' He was starting to look stressed.

'If Luke's left our *LAH* universe and travelled to this other universe,' Stefania explained, 'he's gone into another Luke's life. If we join him, we'll be going into that life with him. We don't know what it'll be, but we should be ready to pretend. You've been lucky . . . in *so* many ways already, Ky. Now we need to be prepared.'

'Yeah,' I agreed, and fixed my most *prepared* face. 'WAIT! There's also these!'

As Stef and Dimi watched, I slid the spindly old Metamorphic Headphones over my ears.

'You know, what you think of as "prepared" worries me . . .' Stef began.

'They're Metamorphic Headphones!' I said. 'They gave us walkie-talkies, and clothes that fitted in with the world last time – OK, we didn't think they'd worked because . . . but they *did*.'

'We've only got one set though,' Stef said.

'Third-party headphones work! You've got your earbuds, right? And Dimi, you've got your headphones?'

'No,' Dimi said.

'Bro, you were just wearing them—'

'No!' Dimi said again. He got to his feet and stared at the floating toy cars, a deep worry on his face. 'We can't go in there.'

'Why not?'

'What if your dad comes in, for one? What's he gonna think if we're missing?'

'We'll just say we were playing hide-and-seek.'

'In this room?!'

'That's what Luke said!' I exclaimed, suddenly defensive of my tiny room. 'Then we say we snuck out. So what? It's not the end of the world.'

'But . . . well . . . Can't we just wait for him?'

'Wait for him?!'

'Yeah!' Dimi said. There was a high, pleading note to his voice. 'He might be out in a minute – won't you, Luke? WON'T YOU, LUKE! COME OUT, LUKE, YOU JUST HAVE TO GET OUT OF THE STUPID SHIP—'

'Whoa, whoa . . .' I began, but Dimi whirled round to confront me.

'We *can't* go into space!' he said. 'We just *can't*. We won't last five minutes! We . . . we have to tell a grown-up about this. This isn't for us.'

Desperately I looked to Stefania for support.

Worryingly, she looked like she thought Dimi was right, but at the same time . . . she didn't. A thought occurred to me. *She wants to go. Not just to help Luke, but to see it. You just have to persuade her.*

'Do you think if we tell the grown-ups they'll look for Luke in a toy racetrack first?' I said. 'NO. My dad would call the police, and they'd send out search parties, and if they *did* listen, they wouldn't go *into* the track. They'd put a big barrier around it, go all Transformers Area 51, and make a big plan to rescue Luke "in six to eight weeks", or "after a government meeting". My fam would be out of a home, and we'd be down a best friend. All because of me,' I added, my voice trailing off.

Dimi had frowned at me when I said the bit about my family being out of a home. I hadn't told them anything, I realised, about Mr Stringer and us maybe having to move out. Had I even properly told Luke? Or had I been too proud to need them, right when I was too scared to go it alone? This was too deep to think about right now. So instead, I came out with the only lie I thought might work.

'And besides,' I said, 'I've already been into space.'

'Serious?' Stef perked up. 'When?'

'Like, one of my first goes!'

'You can fly a spaceship,' Dimi said, flatly suspicious.

'Mm-hmm.' I nodded, thinking *I'm going to regret this.* 'It's easy! It's the only way, Dimi. Please.'

Before Dimi could respond, my bedroom door rattled open, and Dad poked his head in, just as I leaped in front of the floating bits of the Infinite Race.

'I've picked up Celestine and we're nipping to the shops. Anyone want anything before I go? Bovril? Rice pudding?' he said hopefully. Then he frowned. 'Where's Luke?'

Dimi stared at my dad. We stared at Dimi. *Please,* I thought, willing him to somehow hear me. *Please don't tell.*

'Hide . . .' Dimi said slowly. 'Hide . . . and . . . *seek*?'

'Hide-and-seek? In here?' Dad frowned, looking around my room. Then he grinned. 'And you haven't found him?! You lot need to up your game. See ya later.' The door closed, and his footsteps stomped down the stairs as he whistled his way out.

'Thanks, Dimi,' I said, but he shook his head, putting his earbuds in, cheeks pinched with worry.

'Let's just get this over with,' he said. And before we could stop him, he had taken the ship from my hands and placed it on to the track.

'WAIT!' I yelled, and gripped his arm . . .

128

Too late. The toy spaceship *rocketed* forwards. We slammed to the floor, and shrank, the room fizzling into the strings of *LAH*, or *DAH*, or whatever this universe was. Stefania rushed towards us, snatching out at my head, which had already shrunk enough for her to grab hold of it with one hand.

'MnF!' I shouted. 'Nn fnnf MMFMFMMF!!' Stefania shrank to my size, and her painfully strong grip loosened, her headphones *glowing* around her head like a mad halo.

'WHAT?!' she shouted.

'We didn't SHUT THE DOOR!' I shouted, but it was too late. High above us in the dissolving bedroom, a figure walked in.

'Dad says I can stay here if I don't bother you,' the figure said. 'Kyan?!'

It was Celestine! She raced towards us, her giant face terrified as she crouched down beside us.

'Kyan!' she shouted again, but her voice sounded muffled. She was dissolving now, along with the rest of the room.

'DON'T tell Mum and Dad. *Please*,' I shouted, 'PLEASE don't tell!'

But I couldn't hear her reply. Instead, from the ship's

129

radio, there was the most horrifying voice I have *ever* heard.

'REGNAD REGNAD! RAELC EHT HTAP FO EHT RESYEG!'

'*Aliens*, fam!' Dimi shouted. '*Aliens* are attacking!'

12

I was sprawled out on cold grey metal, staring at cables and pipes dangling from the ceiling. The floor *hummed*, like our car on the motorway. There was little space – most of it taken up by the huge, empty docking station in the middle of the ship – it was dark, and the windows were dirty. Basically, it was the type of ship they have in games where angry aliens eat the crew.

'REGNAD REGNAD! RAELC EHT RESYEG!' an angry alien voice blared at us through the distorted speakers above me.

'This is just *brilliant*,' Stefania said. She was now wearing a white, military-looking suit, and wasn't being sarcastic, which was nuts. She stared through the huge

front window at a ginormous, puke-coloured planet in the distance. A huge red spot swirled in the middle, and a misty red ring surrounded one side where the sun peeked around it. Much closer to us was a moon – not *our* moon, but an icy moon the colour of bubblegum ice lollies, brown lines shaking and slashing across it like Mum does to her posh colouring books when she makes a mistake.

'It's Europa,' Stef said, awestruck. 'That moon's Europa, and in the distance . . . that's Jupiter. We're in space.'

And so were the aliens.

'ESAELP POTS GNILAETS RUO RETAW!' the sludgy voice bellowed. Dimi ran to a smaller window at the side of the ship, mouth gaping.

'Oh my days, these freaks look *dodge*,' he said. 'And their spaceship's wet!'

'Oh, *think*, Dimi,' Stefania scoffed, as we hurried to join him. 'Spaceships can't be . . .'

But Dimi was right. Tendrils of green slime trickled in and out of the alien ship, like snot on a mission. Brown, snake-like creatures slithered across its surface too, tangling together into a wriggling mass every time the ship turned, as though they were helping to steer. Even the ship's hull looked nasty; a huge, speckly rock that seemed to have been snapped off some massive ocean reef – not the pretty coral reefs Grandma's shown me in pictures of Jamaica, but the harsh, jagged rocks that cut your ankle open when you trip over a shopping trolley somebody chucked off Southend Pier. (I'm still bitter, all right?) We were up against monsters. Mind-bendingly, bone-shakingly *nightmarish* monsters.

Stefania hurried to a tablet that was hanging from a string near the main viewscreen. On it was this basic screen saver, a home-made logo bouncing around the screen, but Stefania swiped up and began to tap furiously.

'What are you doing?' I asked.

'We have to locate Luke,' she replied. 'Perhaps the ship's computer can tell us where his scout ship is.'

'Ship's computer?' Dimi snorted. 'This ain't *Star Trek.*'

'*Ship's computer activated,*' a *Star Trek*-sounding voice said. '*Welcome to the Europa Quest, demolition ship for the Happy Corporation!*' With a smirk, Stefania scrolled through the tablet's menu. There were several options: MISSION CONTROL, ACTIVATE CONTROLS, EUROPA SCOUT SHIP LOCATION and . . .

'*Europa Scout!*' I said. 'That's the name of the ship that docks into this one, the toy ship Luke's on!' Stefania tapped the screen and it changed, to show a 3D map, our ship and the pale moon below us. There was a dot on the surface of the moon. It was marked OUTERSPACEMAN LUKE.

'You're right!' I said, and scoured the moon ahead of us. 'Luke's in the scout ship! Only . . . I can't see it on the moon.'

We each ran to different windows, looking for Luke's ship, desperate to spot where he'd landed (*or crashed*, I

134

didn't dare think). But the surface was bare, no crashed ships, no Luke. Just a slashed-up desert.

'REGNAD REGNAD! RAELC EHT RESYEG!' the aliens screamed, sounding more furious than ever. Their ship approached ours, and the wriggling mass of brown snakes on its slimy rock-hull moved to the side closest to us. With a wet *belch*, four of the brown snakes were fired out towards us, stretching through the space and sticking *thud-thud-thud-thud* into ours.

'They've webbed us!' Dimi screamed. 'With snakes!'

'Kyan, take evasive action!' Stefania bellowed.

Oh no.

With my claim that I'd flown a spaceship before – '*It's easy!*' – echoing through my head, I ran to the ship's controls. There was a joystick and, next to it, a throttle, *neither* of which did anything when I moved them. Around those useless controls was a panel of roughly six million switches and levers. Desperately I looked for anything marked GO . . . then blindly flicked as many switches as I could, praying the twins wouldn't twig what was making all those alarms blare, those extra wings shoot out of the side and back in, and . . .

'Oh, COME on!' I muttered, as a huge pair of wipers flicked back and forth across every window for the second time that day. Dimi gave me a puzzled look, and I was about to spout some made-up space jargon about having to clean off space-dust or space-rain or space-icicles (*spacicles?*), when another voice came through the radio.

It wasn't the aliens.

It was worse.

'Team Quest, Team Quest, do you read me? This is Chief Stringer of the good ship *Delight*.'

'*Chief* Stringer?' I groaned. 'He was bad enough when he was Officer Stringer!'

'Who is he?' Stef asked.

'He's our –' I nearly said *landlord*, then didn't – '*my* enemy, or at least he has been in every other universe. He keeps getting promoted an' all. My mum says people like him always fail up.'

Suddenly Rule One made sense. I had Hopped into another dimension, had Bumped the Kyan from this dimension into stasis. Now my 'cosmic twin' was suspended in the strings, completely unaware that I was down here talking to his boss Chief Stringer, who in *my* universe was our landlord *Mr* Stringer! Part of me wondered what kind of person this Kyan was. (Part of me wondered again what had happened to the last Kyan I'd left tumbling from that stolen police car in Crooklyn.) Then part of me wondered what kind of person Chief Stringer was, because something weird happened. He said something *nice*.

'We're coming to help you right now, Pilot Kyan. You'll be able to boost down and save your friend, I promise.'

'What does he mean, boost down?' I said. 'Boost down where?'

'I don't know,' Stef said. 'This map says Luke is literally on that moon below us, but I can't see him.'

'Er . . . guys?' Dimi called out nervously. 'How are we going to go anywhere with those things stuck to us?'

He was right. The sucky tentacles were pulling us ever closer, and I could see what looked like the alien ship's wobbly belly *opening up*, as if making room for a snack. The aliens screamed again, and I could've sworn they sounded hungry.

'ESAELP, RUOY DNEIRF DEPLEH SU, WON EW TNAW OT PLEH MIH . . .'

'Pilot Kyan, this is Chief Stringer, do you read me?'

'Maybe he isn't your enemy here?' Stef said. 'We need to reply. Where are the radio controls?'

'On it!' I shouted, but I wasn't. Literally nothing looked like a radio on this stupid dash.

'Wait,' I said. 'In the last world, the Metamorphic Headphones turned into—'

137

I was cut off by the almighty red FLASH of a giant laser cannon SMASHING into the monsters' ship. The snot-snakes gripping us were blown clear, drifting harmlessly away as the ship's snakes slithered around to propel the ship away from us. We'd been saved! A shadow draped across our left, and I ran to see the ship that had rescued us.

'It's them!' I shouted. 'It's the good ship *Delight*!'

It was a *proper* battle cruiser! Painted on every side were stars and eagles and crowns, glittering under the ship's lights. Written across the bottom of the ship, in glowing orange letters that flickered like bonfires, was the word *DELIGHT*. I know you can't hear anything in space, but man! Right then? Trumpets were playing in my head.

'Everyone safe in there?' the Chief's voice boomed. 'I know you're just a demolition team, but are you ready to save your friend from those vicious Erie?'

'I'm ready!' I shouted back. There was a pause, then the Chief came through again, sounding uncertain.

'*Europa Quest*, do you read me? I think . . .' He spoke away from the radio to somebody else. 'I think we may have lost comms.'

'Answer him!' Stefania hissed.

'The Metamorphic Headphones!' I said. 'Last time they

138

turned into a radio, but ...' We all patted the shoulders and necks of our uniforms, but I couldn't feel anything.

'They'll – they'll be firing their geysers soon,' Chief Stringer said, sounding worried. 'If you can hear me, Pilot Kyan, be ready to take that dive.'

'Geezers!' Dimi hissed. 'Your dad was telling my mum about some geezers singing outside your flat late at night, Kyan. Maybe it's them!'

'Not geezers,' Stefania said, fear crossing her face. '*G-e-y-sers*. Europa Moon is full of water, so much that it bursts out in streams called geysers. Maybe ... maybe these aliens have turned them into a weapon.'

Right on cue, the ice on the moon below us began to shake. A gigantic slash appeared, cracking the ice like a creature was about to burst out, getting thicker and more violent as it travelled along the moon's surface, until it stopped – directly below the good ship *Delight*.

'REGNAD REGNAD! RAELC EHT RESYEG!' the sludge-monster screamed again. And like the biggest water pistol in the universe, a jet of water exploded out from Europa and battered the *Delight*. The glass crowns and solar panels that decorated its hull shattered into a thousand fragments, and our heroic battleship was sent spinning back away from us.

'We're hit! We're hit!' Chief Stringer shouted. 'I've got to get out of range, Pilot Kyan. I don't know if you copy, but prepare to take that dive!'

Take that dive? I thought, and felt the sweat prickle my brow as the twins nodded to me. *You've got this.* But before I could confess that I *really* didn't, the geyser began to *move*, this time headed straight for us.

'Kyan, retreat,' Dimi said, his voice getting higher. 'RETREAT, RETREAT!'

I was already trying. Frantic, I flipped every switch, turned every dial and bashed every button. Indicator lights switched on, then off. Heaters came on full blast, froze one side of the ship and melted the other, *again* like our family car. I did everything I could, all too aware that Stef and Dimi were staring at me, a look of growing shock and understanding on their faces. Finally, I closed my eyes, and fought back tears. Shards of the *Delight's* glittering hull floated silently past us like confetti. We didn't stand a chance.

'Dude . . .' said Dimi. 'Can you . . . Can you not fly a spaceship?'

'He lied,' Stefania said, her voice colder than I'd ever heard it. 'He's a noob and *he actually lied.*' I opened my eyes and looked at my friends, trying desperately to think of something to say. But I couldn't. As I watched the geyser burst out of the moon's surface, spelling our certain doom, all I could think about was how I'd failed my three best friends, not only by lying but also losing – and probably killing – them in some other dimension. The deadly cannon of water rocketed towards us, taking up more and more of our viewer until everything was a foaming, frothing, icy blue, and I knew. This was it. This was our end, our doom, our everlasting . . .

'Uhhhh, is it going away?' Dimi said.

I opened my eyes. For a moment the geyser seemed to hover in front of us. Then, as suddenly as it had burst upwards, the water stopped pumping out, and drifted off into space.

'You're right!' Stefania shouted, swiping through screens on her tablet till she reached a dial flashing red, then amber. 'Decreasing water pressure detected!'

'It's run out!' shouted Dimi, and he jumped into the air, punching his fist like he'd just scored a hat trick. 'IT'S RUN OUT! IT'S RUN OUT! THERE AIN'T NO DOUBT, COS IT'S RUN OUT!'

'Good ship *Delight* to Pilot Kyan.' Another familiar voice crackled through the speakers above us. 'This is Navigator Sima. My coordinates were spot on as ever, just out of their range. Your boost opening is ready.'

'Do you know her?' asked Dimi.

'Sima,' I said. 'Kind of. She . . . she was in the other universes. I don't know her from *my* universe though.'

'*Delight* to Pilot Kyan,' Navigator Sima snapped. She sounded *grumpy* in this universe. 'Your path is *clear*. Fire the boosters, over!'

'What path?' said Stefania. I stared at the geyser as it retreated back into the icy moon. It left behind a small, ship-sized tunnel in the moon's surface. That tunnel gave me an idea.

'You said Luke is down there,' I said to Stefania, looking to the map showing the dot of his ship on the moon. 'And their spaceship is wet.'

Stefania stared back at me, cottoning on.

'Maybe this isn't a spaceship,' she said. 'Maybe it's a—'

'Submarine,' I finished. I scoured the controls, eyes roaming across buttons marked OXYGEN LEVELS and STRAFE and EJECT ALL CREW. At the same time Stefania swiped across screens looking for the manual, swooshing past maps, blueprints, some 'MOST WANTED' pictures of two criminals that I *honestly* think might've been this dimension's version of my grandma and her friend Christine . . .

'Yo,' said Dimi. 'What I miss?'

'This ship isn't a flyer,' I said. 'It's a swimmer.'

'Luke's *under the surface*,' Stef added. 'We need something to fire us into that tunnel left by the geyser before the surface freezes back over.'

'Boost!' grumpy Navigator Sima shouted. 'It's now or never!' Brownish pink ice began to form around the hole in Europa's surface.

'It should be obvious,' I said. 'It might say Boost or Turbo or—'

'Superspeed,' Stefania said. 'Or, or . . .'

'High Velocity Powdered Aluminium Jettison?' said Dimi.

'Yeah, I mean that's long ting,' I said, copying my mum, 'but . . . What?'

I looked up. Dimi reached past to point at the throttle in the middle of the console. There, beneath a clear cap, was a red button, badly lit, like it was on but the bulb needed changing. On it, in tiny capitals, were the words HIGH VELOCITY POWDERED ALUMINIUM JETTISON SWITCH.

'*Și pluteam!!*' he sang with a grin, and stabbed it with his finger.

'Dimi, wait—'

BOOSHHHH!! The Formula One car was a donkey ride compared to this rocket! My eyelids wrapped around the back of my head. An elephant sat on my chest.

And the hole in Europa's surface looked *too small*.

Still, our spaceship hurtled down through the tunnel, into the frozen moon. All around us, ice was forming, a shrinking crystalline tunnel that scratched sparks from every side of the hull. In the distance was a pale blue hole, but that hole was shrinking *too* fast.

'*IMPACT WARNING! IMPACT WARNING!*' the ship's computer said, and her Alexa-voice sounded *terrifyingly* scared. The ship juddered and tore, the pale blue exit shrank into a pinhole, then . . . it *disappeared*.

'Nrgh,' I said, face pulled back and jaw clenched too tight to say, *No. Please, no . . .*

Then a CRASH sent us *tumbling* to the floor.

There was a blissful three seconds of pale blue nothing.

'Urgh, that hurt—' Dimi began . . .

Then a wet SPLASH sent us all flying again, and everything turned to black.

13

'Pilot Kyan, come in?'

yiiiiiiiiiiiiiiiiiiiiiiipppppeeeeeee!!!!!!!

'Pilot Kyan, come in?'

wwwwwwahahahaha!!!!!

'Pilot Kyan, come in,' Chief Stringer was whispering through the intercom. 'Pilot Kyan, *please* respond.'

'Ohhhh.' I groaned and opened my eyes. My head *hurt*. Something was digging into my hip. We were swaying backwards and forwards with the ocean, my stomach churning while around us the hull of this space-submarine (*spacemarine?*) groaned and yawned. I staggered to my feet, my head spinning, and reached into my pocket to see what had dug into my side. It was a small black earbud, a bit like Dimi's except longer. Still woozy, I put it back into my pocket and focused on keeping my breakfast in my stomach.

'Pilot Kyan? Science Officer Stefania?' Chief Stringer pleaded. 'Please let me hear that you're OK. Do you think they're hurt?' he added, away from the microphone.

'They deserve to be,' Sima snapped in an angry whisper. 'Leaving it so late to hole-boost that they land in a monster pit.'

yiiiiiiiiiiiiiiiiiiiiiiipppppeeeeeee!!!!!!!

'Wassat?' Dimi said, groggily getting to his feet.

wwwwwwwahahahahaha!!!!!

'That!' Dimi said. 'Tell me you can hear that—'

'*Shh!*' said Stefania. She was frowning at her tablet, at a map of what looked like a gigantic sea, using two fingers to zoom into a red dot marked *EUROPA QUEST*. We were slap bang in the middle of a darker patch of the map, the colour of dried blood.

'Where are we?' I whispered.

'It's called . . .' Stefania looked up at me, her face blanching. 'It's called the Writhing Nest.'

I swallowed. Nothing about that sounded good. I peered through the window. The water was almost pitch-black. Dark, warped shapes bobbed gently in the distance.

Slimy seaweed tumbled across the window, *breathing* as it did, small teeth at the end of each strand nibbling at the glass before it drifted away. I heard strange, watery knocks on every side of the ship's hull, and for a moment we all stood and listened, petrified. Then some sea creature gave out a –

SCREEAAAAM!

– and the terror slapped my senses awake.

'That earbud,' I said, shaking my head clear. 'The Metamorphic Headphones. Search your pockets for an earbud. I think . . . I think it's—'

Amazed, Stef and Dimi patted their pockets, both finding earbuds as I held mine gingerly up to my ear. With a hiss of air, it expanded, opening up to circle the back of my head like a silver floating headband!

'Holonetic Helmet activated,' the ship's computer said *inside* my head. 'Oxygen levels full, pressure stabilisation full. Communications active.'

'Uh . . . hello?' I said shakily. 'This is Pilot Kyan?'

'Oh, what a relief! Good to hear your voice, Pilot!' Chief Stringer said. It was *crazy* how different he was in this universe. 'Our tracking device shows that you're in the Writhing Nest. Are your underwater controls working? You need to make the stream without being eaten.'

'Good idea,' I said decisively, and reached for the throttle, relieved that I'd played that jetbike game for five minutes at the caravan park last summer holiday.

But before I could push it up, Stefania snatched the earbud from my ear. With another hiss, my Holonetic Helmet folded back into it.

'You lied to us, Kyan,' she said flatly. 'We could've died. You put our lives in danger.'

I'd guessed they'd be annoyed. But somehow this took me by surprise. I looked to Dimi – chilled Dimi, who takes nothing too seriously – and he nodded.

'She's right, bro. We need to know – can you actually get us out of this? Cos if you've lied to us twice, that's kinda *de neiertat*.'

'Unforgivable,' Stefania repeated. 'More unforgivable than us leaving this submarine and letting the strings take us home, where we can find somebody else to save Luke.'

I took a deep breath, and looked down at the controls. There was so much I wanted to say. I wanted to tell them what it meant to have them with me when we went back into the Infinite Race together to save our friend. I wanted to describe the guilt weighing me down today, but also the *panic* I'd felt yesterday, about how terrified I was that Mr Stringer would make us move away and I'd never see them any more if I didn't somehow win that prize money. And most of all, I wanted to say that I was sorry, *so* sorry, for all of this.

But I couldn't find the words. I gripped the joystick, and felt a resistance, like it was *doing* something now. It was different to the cars, yes. But it still felt like something I could control.

'You're right,' I said finally. 'I did lie. But I can do this. I *promise* I can do this. PLEASE. PLEASE let me. We have *got* to save Luke.'

Stefania stared at me for a moment, and looked to Dimi. He nodded, and she was about to hand the earbud back to me when she paused.

'Don't you two get chatty with Chief Stringer,' she warned. 'If he guesses we're not from this universe, he might think *we're* the bad guys.'

Nodding, I took the earbud. Once in my ear, it unfolded around my head.

'We're ready. We're going to do this.'

'Thatta boy, Kyan,' Chief Stringer said. 'We'll save your friend, and we'll give those Erie a message not to mess with you again.'

'Why *are* they messing with us?' Stefania demanded, before Dimi mouthed, *I thought we were weren't talking?*

with waving hands and an outraged face. Stefania reddened, but the Chief *did* answer her question.

'I see I can't put much past Science Officer Anev,' he said with a sigh. 'There's no point in denying it. As you know, the Happy Corporation is a simple charity, helping to educate the poorest, most helpless species in the galaxy. As the demolition team yourselves, you have *seen* the amount of wasteland we clear to build schools and hospitals for backward aliens with horrible lives. For a while, it seemed that we might be able to help the Erie. But sadly, some creatures are just too violent to save. No matter how we helped them, the Erie soon turned savage towards us. I sent Outerspaceman Luke to meet with them, hoping that he would be able to calm them down. Instead, they have shot down his ship, and are holding him hostage in our supply pipe.'

'They need to be stopped,' I said grimly.

'Huh,' Sima scoffed. 'Big talk, fly boy. What the Chief is *trying* to say is that you are trapped on a planet where everybody and everything wants to kill you. If you want to live, you need to do exactly what I say – understand?'

'Er, OK – understand.'

'Good. Now, thanks to your showing off, you have landed in the Writhing Nest, *surrounded* by monsters who think you'll go well with rice and a salad. But if you listen, you can hear the yippee stream approaching on your left.'

yiiiiiiiiiiiiiiiiiiiiiipppppeeeeeee!!!!!!!

'Yup,' I said, and took the headband off my head for a moment so I could ask Stef a question without raising Sima's suspicion. 'What *is* that yippee stream?' I muttered to her.

Already on it, Stef mouthed, tapping furiously at her tablet. I put the headband back on.

'Once you've located the stream,' Sima continued, 'you want to accelerate as slowly as possible towards it. Remember, these monsters can't see you, but they can hear you.'

'They can't see me? Can I put my headlights on then?'

'Not yet!' she snapped. 'Remember your training! Headlights are far too noisy! You can put them on at the very last minute.'

'Right,' I breathed. This was it. As slowly, as gently as I could, I pushed the throttle forwards. The ship's motor hummed a bit, but as I stopped pushing, it quietened down again, and we moved forwards, being as quiet as we could be.

You know what people *don't* tell you about exploring underwater moon worlds? They. Are. Scary. Strange masses drifted slowly past us. Some were shaped like our ship, only they were smashed and desolate, their crew long dead and digested. Others were huge, hanging in the distance like enormous wasp nests, teeming with bug-like creatures darting in and out. Unseen critters knocked spookily on every side of our hull, while still those strange sounds zipped past us, sounding distorted and deranged through the water.

yiiiiiiiiiiiiiiiiiiiiippppeeeeeee!!!!!!!
wwwwwwwahooooooo!!!!!

'I've found something about the yippee stream,' Stef whispered. I pulled out my Holonetic Earbud, grateful for the distraction . . . and then saw her screen. *The Erie*, the title was, and it showed a picture of an evil-looking swamp-person, with no eyes and a cavernous, too-wide mouth.

'According to this,' Stefania continued, '*the Erie never evolved to see* like we do. Instead, they use all of the sound around them. Everything in this ocean talks to each other to say what's happening and to warn about potential threats. These streams, the yippee and the wahoo, are a kind of underwater motorway, fast streams of water that make a sound so the Erie know where they are.'

Tooodleoodleooooooh!

'Was that it?' I whispered.

'That's the toodle-oo bypass,' Stefania said. 'According to this, it means we're close to the yippee stream.'

Just then I heard a voice coming through the earbud. As I put it back in my ear, Sima was saying the same thing.

'You're getting close. You'll have to use the changes in its sound as you get near it to listen your way on. Can you do that?'

yiiiiiiiiiiiiiiiiiiiiiippppeee!!!!!!!

' . . . I can't hear any difference,' I said.

'Me neither,' said Stefania. But Dimi stepped forwards excitedly.

'I can!' he exclaimed. 'It's ahead, but we need to aim a little bit right and go a bit deeper. A little bit more. More,' he said, then, 'STOP! Now can you hear it?'

yiiiiiiiiiiiiiiiiiiiiiippppeee!!!!!!!

He was right. The next yippee that shot past sounded noticeably louder and higher. We'd always made fun of how Dimi was into the *next* tune, listening them to death before moving on to the next. We'd never thought about how amazing it was that he learned the lyrics so quickly, or how you could play him the start of any track and he'd know it, but I *seriously* appreciated it right now.

'Now,' Dimi said. 'If we move a *bit* backwards, we'll hit it.'

'Exactly right, Toilet Technician Dimi!' Sima said approvingly. 'Good ears!'

'Thanks,' Dimi said proudly, then paused. 'What did you call me?'

'Now, as he says, Pilot Kyan,' Sima continued, 'ease backwards. Remember, we *won't* be able to radio you while you're on the stream. You'll be on your own.'

'OK,' I said. I pulled the throttle back slightly. Thrusters burst gently from the front of the ship, and . . .

CLANG.

We'd ground to a halt. I pushed the lever a little bit harder, and the engine revved, painfully loud. Still we didn't move.

'What do I do?' I said, trying to keep my voice from quavering. Beads of sweat formed on my nose.

'Errrr . . .' Sima said. 'Go forwards a bit, of course! You're probably stuck in a reef.'

I pulled the lever back, pulling the ship backwards, then . . .

CLANG.

We were dead in the water. There was silence, just my quickened breathing, and the light drip of a sweat drop falling from my nose to the metal floor.

'OK, Kyan,' Chief Stringer whispered. 'Nothing to worry about. You're alongside the yippee stream. If you switch on your headlights, you'll be able to see what you're snagged on, and you can get away.'

So I did.

'AAAAAAAAAARGHHHHH!' we all screamed. Six beams of light flooded out from the ship, aimed directly into the razor-sharp, bloodstained teeth of the biggest, most *roadman* squid I'd ever seen! It had no gigantic eye, but instead its mouth stretched out to the top of its head, wide enough to snap those teeth down and make deep dents in the front of our hull. I slammed the joystick left, accelerating away as fast as I could, but it lashed out at us

with six of its twelve tentacles, its suckers sticking to our windows with a horrible squelch. I rammed the throttle to full, pulling us almost free but not quite . . .

'Stop!' Dimi shouted suddenly, and I was so surprised, I did.

'The stream is coming behind us,' he whispered. 'Wait till I say go.'

So we sat there. And as we did, shapes began forming in the depths. They multiplied, grew bigger, closer. Squinting into the hazy light, I made out a gang of the gnarliest, scabbiest, most *killer-est* sea beasts I could've ever imagined. They were headed for us; shivering jellyfish the colour of bleeding hearts, giant eels that crackled and *frenzied* with electricity, and, at the head of the pack, an enormous, *ginormous* white shark, with no eyes and row after row of grinning, oversized teeth.

A figure sat upon that shark.

'That . . .' Stefania whispered, and pointed a barely trembling finger at it. 'That's one of the Erie.'

The picture on her tablet hadn't done it justice. This thing was *way* scarier. Instead of clothes, the Erie was covered in the toothy seaweed that had nibbled our window. Tiny worms crawled across its body, moving with it in the same way those huge snakes had roamed across the Erie ship. On its hands and feet were deadly-looking claws, but what made my skin truly crawl was the Erie's face. It had no eyes, no nose. At the centre was that mouth, continuously moving, opening so wide it practically took up the Erie's entire head, before shrinking into what looked like a cat's bum. (Soz, but it *did*.)

The Erie lifted one swamp-green arm to point right at us, and from its throat came an ear-splitting shriek – a dolphin crossed with a wet burp crossed with a fork scratching across a plate.

'LUFERAC! I MA GNIOG OT EVOMER EHT SELCATNET!'

'Dimi, where's that stream?' I whispered. I glanced towards him, but his eyes were closed in concentration, one finger held up. The squid tightened its grip, our hull creaked, and all the monsters of the moon prepared to feast.

'Dimi!' Stefania hissed. 'Stop feeling the Force and tell us when we can—'

'GO!!' Dimi shouted, and I *wrenched* the accelerator down, firing forward thrusters that knocked the Erie's shark back. We were propelled backwards, our hull wrenching horribly under the squid's tight grip, but it wasn't enough, I *knew* it wasn't enough and –

Yiiiiiiiiiiiiiiiiiipppppeeeeeee!!!!!!!!

We *harpooned* through the water, blasted by a stream I couldn't even see! The squid's tentacles *pop-pop-pop-popped* off the window, it tumbled away into the deep, and all of us whooped with relief!

'You did it!' Stef shouted, and hugged her brother. 'Toilet Cleaner Dimi did it!'

'Toilet Technician, yeah? Don't disrespect my lane,' Dimi said, but he was grinning wide. I felt happy to be alive, happier still that my friends were alive with me. We'd save Luke, I was sure of it. Nothing could stop us.

'H2-oh no, octopus!' I yelled. 'We're taking the yippee road!'

Cringe. That hadn't sounded as corny in my head. The others fell silent and I remembered that I had lied to them, had landed both them *and* Luke in this whole horror game of a situation. Would they ever be my friends again?

Finally, Stef spoke up.

'It can't be an octopus, it had twelve tentacles,' she said, and paused. 'It's a dodecaheccapus.'

I glanced at her, and she gave a small smile. We were sort of friends again.

'I don't know who's more tragic,' grumbled Dimi. 'Youse lot are geeks.'

14

Once on the yippee stream, the red dot of our ship zipped along, away from the Writhing Nest and along the map towards 'Outerspaceman Luke'. The dark waters outside became a foamy-white blur, and as Dimi went to the toilet and Stef browsed the ship's tablet, I looked closer around the ship.

It was *ropy*; rusted metal grilles, faulty, flickering lights and more sticky-tape repairs than you'd want on a space-ship *or* a submarine. There weren't any proper chairs by the control panels, just these standing back-rests that dug into my butt and my spine at the same time. Here and there were these random poles to hold on to, like on a bus, and I half expected to see a button for the bell sticking out of them. The toilets were at the back, two cubicles with a sign on the door: *WARNING! FLUSHING BOTH TOILETS WITHIN TEN SECONDS MAY CAUSE DANGEROUS ACCELERATION AND HULL DISINTEGRATION.*

Dimi opened the door now, and pointed up at the sign.

'Even flushing the toilet kills you in this hellhole!' he moaned.

Still, though, there *were* little pieces of home everywhere; a darts-looking holographic board with a mini-league below it ('SHOOTER ANEV' was winning); a fridge stocked with nothing but a cake box and a note that said: 'EXCRUCIATING PAIN FOR ANYONE WHO EATS THIS CAKE' (I *think* it was Other Stefania's). Then I saw a photograph tacked on the fridge door, and with a start I realised it was *us*, our cosmic twins.

They were grown-ups, proper different in some ways, but I could guess who everyone was. There was Other Dimi, looking flash in this ridiculous-looking light-up suit that I bet cost all his wages. There was Other Stefania, wearing a buzz cut, looking up from the tablet like she was about to swear at whoever was taking the photograph. There was Other Me, a dapper dude in my pilot's gear – he looked a *bit* more cocky than I would've liked (plus he reminded me of Other Kyan back in Crooklyn, which I didn't want to think about right then). So instead I moved on to Other Luke, still looking both older *and* younger than the rest of us somehow, wearing a beaming-wide smile on his face that summed up how I reckon all our cosmic twins were feeling right then.

He was happy, he was chill. He was with his friends.

With a sudden lump in my throat, I turned to say something to the others – then a warning beep sounded from the main viewscreen.

'We're here,' said Stefania.

My nerves suddenly jangled again. I walked back to the joystick and gripped it. For one pants-wetting moment I realised that nobody had said *how* you leave a slipstream. But as I tilted the joystick, the ship came up against a soft, invisible barrier . . . then pushed smoothly through it, slowing to a much gentler speed. I took a deep breath of relief . . . and like the sea was matching my calm, the ship filled with a warm, cosy light.

'Here's *nice*,' Dimi breathed. He was right. There was no monster's nest in this part of Europa. The waters here were paradise clear, lit up like a swimming pool by lights that twinkled as they floated by. The seabed was made up of sparkling crystals, a diamond dance floor that seemed to go on forever, and the music was the soft, muffled sound of unseen currents moving gently, harmlessly around us. It was like the universe's biggest, *bestest* aquarium.

'Yeah,' Stefania said, a frown on her face, 'but there's nothing *alive* here. Where's all the fish? Where's all the schools and hospitals Chief Stringer was building?'

Nobody had an answer for that. According to our viewscreen map, the *Quest* had left the slipstream on the other side of Outerspaceman Luke, so I tilted the joystick – still nervous about these controls – and turned us around in a long, sweeping arc. We passed over the yippee stream, which in these bright waters was a wispy white road of froth. And then, slowly, massively, a *ginormous* vertical pipe came into view, hanging down the waters ahead, the kind of pipe Super Mario would *choom-choom-choom* down if he was the size of a skyscraper.

'What is *that*?' Dimi said, awestruck.

'It must be the supply pipe,' Stefania said. 'The one Chief Stringer said the Erie blocked. The one Luke is trapped inside.'

It was as wide as at least four *Europa Quest*s, a circular pipe made from a metal so polished I could see the *Quest*'s reflection as we approached it. It stretched up and up, so far that it disappeared into the sparkling waters above us.

But the bottom of the pipe hung straight ahead, suspended a hundred metres above the crystal seabed. Except . . .

'Look,' Stefania muttered, pointing down. In the seabed directly beneath the pipe there was a massive, blackened crater. Easing the joystick forwards and pulling back on the throttle, I swooped the ship to a stop directly between the pipe and the jagged, scorched hole beneath it. The temperature increased, as though the water outside was warmer, and there was a funny, bitter smell, like something had been burning that shouldn't burn.

'Something's exploded here, something *big*,' Stefania said, craning to look up through the top of the viewscreen. 'What's happened to the pipe?'

Could this ship turn without thrusters? I didn't think so, but held on to a bus pole and pulled back the joystick to see. To my surprise, the ship rotated, the floor tipped up, my butt fell back comfortably into the standing chair and . . .

BANG! Something slammed to the floor behind me.

'You couldn't warn me?' Dimi groaned, gripping on to the bus poles and clambering to his feet.

'Sorry,' I said with a grin. 'I guess that's what the poles and seats are for.'

My grin faded though as I looked up at the opening of

the pipe. It was *wrecked*, all gnarled and snarled and warped, the metal buckled and blown back. And, just as Chief Stringer had described, the pipe was packed full of huge crystal shards that were blackened and scorched too.

'Luke's trapped behind all that rubble,' I said, my mouth dry. 'I hope . . . I hope he's still—'

'*Europa Quest*, can you hear me?' Chief Stringer asked.

'I can hear you,' I said tersely. 'We're at the supply pipe. There's no sign of any Erie.'

'They're there somewhere,' the Chief said with certainty. 'We just picked up this video. Other Luke must've tried to send it to us, but whatever blocking devices the Erie are using have garbled the video. Still, it's pretty rough.'

A video came up on the viewscreen. It was a video of Luke, the *other* Luke. He was making a selfie from within his scout ship, his viewscreen behind him. The video kept glitching forwards with a loud static *BSSH!* that made me wince.

'I hope you get this . . .' Other Luke said, and – *BSSH!* – the video skipped forwards.

'. . . this Erie's right behind me—'

BSSH!

'. . . threatened to blast me out of the water if I don't stop. I *won't* stop though—'

164

BSSH!

'. . . got to do what's right—'

BSSH!

On the next glitch forwards we all gasped. For stuck against the viewscreen, staring at us behind Luke, was an Erie, brandishing a long, sword-like weapon. There was the sound of an explosion, and Other Luke spun around horrified in his chair. I let out a 'NO!' . . .

And the video cut to black.

'Did you watch it?' the Chief asked.

'We did,' I said, my teeth gritted with fury. 'What do they even want? Why have they blocked him in there?'

'Who knows what they want,' Stringer said sadly. 'When a species gets as hateful and vicious as this, all we can do is fight for what is right.'

I nodded in agreement, and looked to Dimi. He looked as angry as I was, but Stefania clambered across the bus poles to a porthole-sized window at the side, and gazed thoughtfully at the smoking crater in the crystal seabed below us.

'Weird,' she said to herself. She turned to me, and took out her Holonetic Earbud before speaking again. 'I thought Chief Stringer said this was a *supply* pipe?'

'So?'

'So, if it was *supplying* stuff, that means things would've been coming *out* of this end. It would've been like a blow-dryer, not a hoover. To explode those massive crystals out of the seabed and then lift them up to block the pipe that's blowing *out* . . . I mean, how did the Erie even do that?'

I turned to look down through the rear-view screen at the crater below us. Another time I might've been interested to know why. But seeing that video – that crystal plug trapping Luke – had sent butterflies of worry and blame fluttering through my chest.

'To be honest,' I said, 'I *really* wanna get my friend back.'

'Me too,' Dimi agreed.

'Me too, Pilot Kyan!' Chief Stringer boomed. 'So what's the delay? Let's activate the gunnery chair, guys, and let your hotshot take down the Erie laser defences!'

'Where's the button?' I said, before I remembered that I was *supposed* to know this stuff. 'Er . . . Toilet Man Dimi, that's a test for you!'

'Always helping the toilet tykes!' Chief Stringer laughed as Dimi shot me evils. 'But probably best to wait till after we've got Outerspaceman Luke safely away for this particular lesson, eh? Flip that red switch and get Sharpshooter Anev on the case!'

Red switch! Looking desperately across the control panel, I found the only red switch on the board and flipped it. With a metallic groan, a rusty old cannon swivelled out of the front side of our ship, a mouldy old office chair clattered out of the cupboard beneath one of the front windows, and a plastic laser tag gun tumbled from the ceiling like an oxygen mask.

'Can there be a *single* universe out there where Kyan Green *doesn't* drive some taped-up wreck?' I whispered.

'Is no matter,' Dimi growled in an action hero voice, 'to Sharpshooter Anev.' He leaped into the chair, gripped the laser gun and *turned around to face us*!

'How'd I look?' he said, as the rusty cannon behind him swung around too.

'FACE FORWARDS!' both me and Stef shouted.

'Oh,' Dimi said, and faced the front. I was starting to remember that Dimi *hates* video games. Did we have the right 'Sharpshooter Anev' here?

'OK, Dimi,' I said cautiously. 'The laser cannons are ahead. If you hold the gunsight to your eye—'

'*Ma-tah ma-tah,*' Dimi roared. 'Let's get 'em!' He blasted wildly, his chair skating away from the viewscreen as the old cannon *PEUNG-PEUNG*ed green bolts of energy that

167

*ping*ed and *brrrumm*ed off the rim of the pipe before bouncing harmlessly off into the deep.

'All right, so it might take a minute,' Dimi said with an embarrassed grin. He fired two more shots that missed the pipe entirely.

'I see what you mean,' Stefania said, not even looking up.

That wound Dimi up. He aimed again, much more carefully, and fired several green blasts at the rock-filled opening of the pipe. OK, so the first three still zipped off into the deep, and the other two weren't exactly bullseyes – not even a double two – but as the bolts of energy struck the rocky plug, a huge shard of crystal broke off it, sinking slowly towards us. They were big – big enough that I had to swerve around them – but when the clouds of dust settled, the pipe was still packed with crystal.

Dimi kept on firing, and soon at least fifty per cent of his shots were hitting the target. The water was cloudy with dust and huge shards of crystal – which provided some good dodging practice for me, to be honest. Driving a spaceship-submarine is *different* from a car. The turns aren't anything like as sharp – something I twigged when we nearly crashed directly into the pipe, and I had to veer away for a long loop-di-loop back around. But then I remembered the buttons I'd seen near the joystick, four arrows around the word STRAFE. Pressing one of these fired thrusters out of the side of the ship, like sidestepping in a shoot 'em up. After dodging one boulder with a strafe and another with a barrel roll, Dimi blasted five shots that all smashed into the rock, and I felt a thrill despite my fears.

'We can do this!' I cried out excitedly. 'I really think we can!'

And then Navigator Sima ruined the party.

'Fly boy,' she said, and there was urgency in her voice. 'You've got company. At least five Erie riding megalodons, and they've brought enough bogeys to burst your nose.'

'She's right,' Dimi said, going pale. 'Look.'

A dark, poisonous-looking cloud was pouring out from the yippee stream. The cloud swarmed towards us, until I could make out the five giant sharks leading it. It was the Erie riding their sharks – or megalodons, as Sima called them – and as their army of sea beasts swarmed closer, as the sound of screams and snapping jaws reached a deafening, water-distorted pitch, as the clear blue sea churned dark and the air turned as cold as night sweat trickling down my spine, that sickening feeling twisted my stomach: the feeling you get when you've made a terrible, terrible mistake.

We were a toy boat dropped in the bath after my dad's used it. Surrounded by grime and hairs and sickening creatures, we had nowhere left to turn.

15

'**U**OY EVAH OT POTS!' the Erie shrieked.

It was the Erie we had encountered before, I was sure of it. Its megalodon swam menacingly towards the *Quest*, as the Erie stood tall on its back like a surfboard. Behind it, around us, hundreds – *thousands* – of sea monsters shrieked and bayed for our blood.

'UOY EVAH OT POTS!'

Already I'd helped land my best friend in peril. Now my other best friends were about to be eaten by a Grab Bag-sized shark, all because I *thought* I was hot stuff with a joystick.

'YRROS TUB UOY TONNAC . . .' the Erie screamed, '*TONNAC* YORTSED TAHT EGAKCOLB!' With a

swoosh of its massive tail, the megalodon propelled towards us, its deadly teeth SNAPPING *millimetres* away from our viewscreen before *woomph*ing up and over us.

'Pilot Kyan,' the Chief said, 'I can't imagine your nerves right now. But if there's *any way* you can get that last layer of rock destroyed, we will find some way to help you, I promise.'

'Thanks, Chief,' I said, 'I appreciate it.' Desperately I looked over to Dimi. He nodded his head, as determined as I was.

'I swear we've nearly broken through the rock, Ky,' he said. 'Right now my shot to that pipe is blocked by a two-headed manta ray, but as soon as it moves . . .'

But before I could say anything else, the Holonetic Earbud was taken from my ear.

'Stefania,' I said, 'I've really got to focus on this now—'

'Look at this,' Stefania said quietly, and gestured to the tablet. 'The words. The language the Erie are using. It . . . I swear it makes *sense* somehow.'

'It's Romanian?!' I said, and she punched my arm.

'Don't be ignorant,' she said. 'No. The ship's computer has written down all the comms from the Erie. Does something seem weird?'

She gave me the tablet. It showed a transcript of all the Erie's words so far.

REGNAD REGNAD RAELC EHT RESYEG
ESAELP POTS GNILAETS RUO RETAW
ESAELP, EW EVAH RUOY DNEIRF EH—
[TRANSMISSION CEASED]

'I dunno,' I said, exasperated. 'Scary alien speak, innit! Why does it . . . ?'

'*Matter,*' I was going to say, but then I paused. Stefania had agreed to carry on with this adventure, even after I'd lied. And . . . and maybe there *was* something strange about those words.

'Maybe . . .' I admitted, 'maybe we were so scared, we didn't try to make sense of what they said. We just escaped, then slapped ourselves on the back, and . . . *backslaps to be slapped back . . .*'

'Eh?' Stefania said, interested.

'Does this tablet have notes?' I said. Stef swiped down from the tablet, and it extended lower to reveal a writing app. I rewrote the first word of the first Erie message on the screen above . . . backwards.

REGNAD
DANGER

'It's *backwards*!' Stef said. 'The words are *backwards*!' She selected all of the sentences and dragged them down to the notepad, rewriting each word below until she had a list:

DANGER! DANGER! CLEAR THE GEYSER!
PLEASE STOP STEALING OUR WATER!
PLEASE, WE HAVE YOUR FRIEND HE—
[TRANSMISSION CEASED]

'Whoa,' I said. 'They were really saying that this whole time?'

'For evil aliens,' Stefania said, 'they say please a *lot*. And *are* we stealing their water?'

'We didn't do nuffink!' I protested.

'I mean our cosmic twins, dum-dum,' Stefania said. 'And they might not've even known. We're a demolition ship, right? So we go around and smash things up, clear rocks and stuff. We probably helped make this part of Europa all pretty and dead. But where are all the schools the Chief said they were building? And what did the Other Luke mean when he said that something was wrong here?'

'Any news, Pilot Kyan?' the Chief said. 'Remember, if you can unblock that pipe we can help you.'

'Yep,' I said, frantically putting my earbud back on. 'Yes, I, er . . . We're still looking for the shot. Just . . . finding the shot.'

'Nearly got it too!' Dimi said, his blaster fixed on the manta ray blocking the pipe. Exchanging a glance with Stefania, I took out my earbud and stepped closer to the viewscreen. She clambered to the front of the ship, tablet in hand, and stood in front of the viewscreen. It seemed to *infuriate* the sea monsters. Their frenzied shrieks filled the air like a bloodthirsty whalesong, and at last the Erie leader lost its patience and *launched* at us, pulling out a murderous-looking sword to swing at the viewscreen . . .

'POTS!' Stefania screamed.

175

'Pots?' I said, bemused. '*Ohhhh* . . .'

And, to my amazement, the Erie *did* stop. The sea monsters stopped shrieking and baring their teeth. The Erie leader paused, mid-swing, then pulled that murderous sword back to its side.

Everybody waited.

Stefania began to write, desperately quickly, on the tablet, while we all held our breath. Behind us Dimi *tch*'d and readjusted his posture – like he'd *almost* had a shot but not *quite*. Finally, Stefania looked up, directly at the Erie's pulsating mouth, and read the words she'd written out loud.

Actually, she *shrieked* them.

'NAC UOY RAEH EM?!'

The Erie stared back at her, and for a long second I thought it would swing that sword again. But instead it made a noise, a noise that sounded suspiciously like a *huh*.

'I NAC RAEH EHT RENNUG KAERB DNIW.'

There was a brief pause, then warbling screams and shrieks burst out across the Erie's thousands of troops. I wasn't sure, but I could've *sworn* they were all laughing.

'Pilot Kyan,' Chief Stringer said, sounding more impatient than before. 'We have lasers inside that pipe. As soon as you clear the blockage they can help to save you all.'

That was strange. He hadn't mentioned the lasers in the pipe before. Still, I didn't answer. I stared at Stefania, frantically rewriting the Erie's recorded words as soon as they showed up on the tablet screen.

'Huh,' she said, just like the Erie alien had, and glanced back to Dimi with a slight smile on her face before frantically writing some more.

'Ky,' Dimi said. He hadn't looked away from the blaster once. 'Ky, I swear that two-headed manta ray's about to sneeze.'

'DESAELP OT TEEM UOY!' Stefania screamed before I could answer. 'YM EMAN SI FETS. UOY ERA GNIKAEPS SDRAWKCAB!'

Suddenly the sea was *silent*. The Erie drifted slowly towards us. Every muscle, every flap of skin, every toothy worm on its body was still, aimed towards us.

'SDRAWKCAB . . .' the Erie shrieked, and paused. Was it me, or was that shriek a bit softer than before? 'SDRAWKCAB.'

'Yes . . .' Dimi said quietly into his earbud. 'Yes, I'm listening, Chief.' *Why's the Chief speaking just to Dimi?* I thought. But then the Erie spoke again, its next words slow and stumbling, as though it was working them out on the go.

'PLEA. SED . . .'

'No, PLEASED!' Stefania said.

'Probably don't need to correct them, Stef,' I said, still nervous.

'PLEASED . . .' the Erie shrieked, 'PLEASED . . . TO . . . MEET . . . YOU.'

'PLEASED TO MEET YOU TOO!' Stef shrieked, and breathed a sigh of relief. The hordes of sea monsters had fallen silent; a watching, deadly army. Then the Erie clamped its mouth to the glass with a loud *THUD* that made both me *and* Stefania yell out in fright. But now *I* was the one starting to make sense of all this.

'Is . . . ?' I said, and walked up to the viewscreen. 'Is that . . . Is that like a fist bump?!' I started to put my mouth on the glass, but Stef punched me on the arm.

'Just talk, you idiot!' she hissed.

'ALL RIGHT?!' I quavered. 'I'M KYAN!'

'MY . . . EMAN . . .' With its lips pulsing against the glass of our viewscreen, the Erie's voice echoed across the ship, making my ribs shake. 'MY NAME SI . . . MY NAME IS . . . MY NAME IS . . . STACEY!'

'Leave off,' I said. Stef punched me again.

Stacey-the-Erie continued.

'YOUR   CHIEF   . . .   SAID   . . .   THE   OTHER

WAY ... WAS BEST ... TO TALK. SDRAWKCAB, NOT ... BACKWARDS.'

There was a long pause, as this sunk in.

'TI ... TI ... IT ... WILL ... BE ... EASIER ... TO ... SHOW ...' Stacey said. 'PUT YOUR MOUTHS ON THE WINDOW TO LINK.'

I gave Stefania the *smuggest* look of the day.

'I *told* you,' I said. 'Urgh!' Gingerly Stefania stepped forwards until we were both close to the viewscreen. My nose scrunched up in distaste as I leaned forwards to kiss the dirty glass. In the background I noticed Dimi was speaking urgently and quietly into his earbud, his eye still trained through his blaster. *Something's wrong*, I thought. *Why is he ... ?*

That's when Everything Went Black.

Only ... it didn't completely. Because suddenly I could *hear*. I was in Europa's ocean, and I could *hear*. The shrieks and wails of the sea monsters, the *yippees* and *wahoos* of zipping slipstreams, I could hear them all again, but this time they all fit. They were all a line or a colour or a shape, and together they all painted a picture, a picture that was – and oi, I don't use this word much – but it was *beautiful*. It was beautiful; more beauty than I could breathe in. Everything – the giant crabs with six pincers, the fish with five jaws, and of course the twelve-tentacled dockerdackerlackerpus – everything just *fit*, and this murky, mouldy, muddy, stormy sea, this whole weird place was *paradise*. Living in it – not *owning* it, but existing peacefully, a *part* of it – were the Erie, and their lives were hard like my mum and dad's are hard, and like my mum and dad their lives were *theirs*, their families were *theirs*, and for a long time it seemed like their homes were *theirs* as well, nobody's to take away.

Then Chief Stringer arrived. He seemed friendly, a lot friendlier than my Mr Stringer anyway. But he told the Erie that he could understand them perfectly when they messaged him, even though they were speaking backwards, and he said that nobody else could understand them because the Erie were *behind*, because the Erie were *slow*, because the Erie needed to *get with the plan*, to get *educated*.

Without really knowing what they were agreeing to, the Erie agreed. That's when the Chief brought us in. Because we thought we were helping (and maybe because we were being paid a lot of money), we helped to clear this part of the Europa seas, zapped it and bulldozed it and blew it up, until all the plant life was cleared all the way back to the crystal seabed, a dead, sparkling desert. Then, once the area was ready, Chief Stringer built what he called his 'supply pipe'.

Then the water level started to drop.

This pipe didn't *supply*, like Chief Stringer had promised. This pipe *took*, pumping gallons and gallons of water off Europa Moon. Alarmed, the Erie tried to contact the Chief, then when he didn't answer they tried to destroy the pipe themselves, only to be attacked by laser cannons or, even worse, sucked up the pipe, never to be seen again. And as the water level dropped, the underwater desert grew.

'I hope ...' Other Luke said, and I gasped because suddenly this vision – er, *hearing* – quest had changed.

I was sitting on the back of a megalodon behind Other Luke's viewscreen. The seas around us were the same empty, endless swimming pool. But instead of a massive crater beneath, there were just a load of metal boxes sitting on the crystal seabed, their lights blinking noisily up at us. Above us, the pipe was *way* lower down, its opening shiny and glimmering instead of the torn, jagged edges it had now. It was clear of any blockage, but it was sucking up water with a constant, powerful *HUM*. I could *feel* the waters trying to drag me up into it, could feel the megalodon's powerful muscles stretch and strain as it grunted in the effort of keeping us safe.

'I hope you get this,' Other Luke said. 'Chief Stringer's blocking all my comms. He's lying to us, gang. He's stealing the Erie's water, and he's making them seem like the bad guys. And OK, they do *seem* scary – I really wish I could understand what they were saying. But look – this Erie's right behind me and hasn't hurt me at all. Chief Stringer, on the other hand . . . he's threatened to blast me out of the water if I don't stop. I *won't* stop though. I've planted mines all along the seabed, as close to the pipe as I can manage without being sucked in myself. I'll get to a safe distance, fire my missiles at the mines, and flush-boost outta there – you remember that move Dimitar came up with, Ky? That got us past *everything*. And OK, I *know* you don't agree with me doing any of this. But *please*, Kyan, *please* just . . . don't worry about the money for a minute. We've got to do what's right.'

Again there was that feeling, shame drenching me like cold rain. Kyan Green had done it again in this universe. I had become so obsessed with money that I'd put it ahead of my friends. But Other Luke sighed, and for a moment I could've sworn *he* looked ashamed.

'I know it's not the same for me to say it . . .' he began – when a bolt of blue energy blasted out of the pipe towards him!

'KOOL TOU!' Stacey screamed. Other Luke turned in shock, firing up the thrusters just in time. The *Europa Scout* darted forwards, and the laser bolts flew down past us . . . right into one of Other Luke's mines! I felt a *CRACK* far below us, then a *deafening* explosion, a bright white noise, screamed through my brain. Muffled *WHOOSH*es flew past us, those huge lumps of blasted crystal sending us spinning back and back and back until I felt sick with dizziness. But even through the pain my hearing – Stacey's hearing – picked up Luke's *Europa Scout*, tumbling up the pipe and smashing into the laser cannon that had shot at him with a horrible *SCREAM* of twisting metal.

Finally, the explosion cleared. I drifted through the water, barely conscious, my ears ringing. And then, somewhere in the distance, I heard a sound coming from inside the pipe. It was a *flash*. The same *flash* I'd heard when the Infinite Race blasted us to other dimensions.

Other Luke was in stasis now. Our Luke was trapped in that pipe.

'KY!' Dimi shouted from somewhere. 'KY, I'VE GOT THE SHOT!'

'Eh?' I muttered. He shouted again, louder, but still from a different place.

'KY! KYAN! I'VE GOT THE SHOT, I'VE GOT THE SHOT . . .'

The soundscape Stacey had created began to melt. The picture of sounds I'd been watching fell away. My vision began to return. And Dimi shouted again.

'KY! KY! THAT MANTA'S GONNA SNEEZE! I'LL HAVE THE SHOT, WHAT DO I DO?'

'Shoot!' the Chief snarled through the radio, and as I snapped back to reality, I saw Dimi pull the trigger before I could even move.

'No, Dimi! WAIT!' I shouted, but it was too late.

It was a perfect shot. The two-headed manta ray sneezed, both its heads going down forwards, and Dimi pulled the trigger three – *peung-peung-peung* – times. Three green bolts blasted out, straight past the other Erie, below and above countless sea monsters, and *just* in through the gap left by the manta ray's bowing heads. They shot through them, past the rest of the army and *SMASHED* into the crystal boulders blocking up the pipe.

'Yesssss!' Chief Stringer shouted through the radio, and my stomach dropped at the sudden *sneer* in his tone. It was the sneer Officer Stringer had, as he smashed us off the road; the sneer Kenneth Tha Goat had, as he blasted Almost-Christine off her bike. It was the sneer Mr Stringer had when he told my parents their rent was going up.

'I knew he'd do it!' Chief Stringer crowed. 'If you want

the wrong thing doing right, get yourself an idiot Toilet Tech!'

'I . . .' Dimi said, horror crossing his face. 'What?'

The smoke cleared from the pipe. There was a small hole in the rock, I saw, right in the middle. Small chips began to pull off it, and the hole grew bigger. As it grew bigger, then *bigger* chips came off, stripping the blockage away faster and faster until the hole was as big as *Europa Quest*.

'IT'S OPEN! THE PIPE IS OPEN AGAIN!' Stacey shrieked, panic in their voice. But then I saw something that, finally, gave me hope.

'LUKE!' I shouted, and pushed the throttle up *full*. The little *Europa Scout* was there, spinning backwards out of the pipe, and as we darted forwards, between desperately fleeing fish and jellyfish and manta rays, I saw Luke through the viewscreen, determinedly and desperately moving the controls. But a current was building, a flow of water into the pipe, and while the scout ship wasn't being dragged up it *yet*, it wasn't able to escape either.

'We've got to get him!' I shouted. 'Stef! Can you work out how to dock our ship with his?'

'Already found it!' Stefania shouted back, and tapped her tablet.

'*Docking sequence activated*,' the ship's computer said. '*Position craft above scout ship.*'

That was easier said than done. Gritting my teeth, I dodged left around a scattering school of terrified piranha-looking fish, strafed right around Stacey-the-Erie, who was trying to marshal them away from the pipe, and winced as a *huge* crystal shard *GRRRRRR*inded alongside our hull.

'Dimi!' I shouted. 'Can you shoot out the boulders while I—?'

'Nu-uh,' Stefania said, then clambered over to the gunnery chair and whacked Dimi on the shoulder. 'Budge up, Dimbag, you're on docking duty. This job needs Sharpshooter Anev.'

'What?!' Dimi retorted. '*I'm* Sharpshooter An—'

Just then he dropped the blaster. It bounced on the trigger, firing a burst from our cannon that bounced back off the rim of the pipe and sparked off our *own hull*.

'Yup, yup,' Dimi said, and gave up the chair.

Well, I've played her at video games. I should've known the type of shot she was. But nothing prepared me for Stefania behind this blaster. With one hand steadying the binoculars, one hand holding the blaster out in front of her, she – *PEUN-PEUN* – took out the next three boulders headed our way, then spun around in her chair to – *PEUN-PEUN* – take out a deadly-looking shard that was about to slice into Stacey-the-Erie.

'Yes!' I shouted, and with the free space I pushed the throttle forwards – then pulled it *right* back as we *shot* forwards, the current into the pipe getting stronger by the second. Luckily, we came to a stop right above Luke's *Europa Scout.*

'*Docking sequence initiated,*' the ship's computer said. '*Turn red lever to open valves.*'

'Red lever . . . where is it?!' I said, panicking.

'I'm on it,' Dimi said, a grim determination in his face. Swinging from bus pole to bus pole, he moved across the ship, around the docking bay, like he was on the monkey bars, until he reached a red lever that stuck out of the side furthest away. Reaching out with just one arm keeping him from falling, Dimi gripped the lever and *hefted* it down.

'*Valves initiated,*' the ship's computer said. '*Turn green lever to open hatch.*'

'Green – where's the green lever?!' I shouted, but Dimi was already swinging back across the docking bay, his expression still the same, like all his anger at Chief Stringer was concentrated in these moves.

'Done!' he shouted. There was the metallic sound of huge doors opening below us, and I felt a spark of hope. *He's nearly there, we've nearly got him, we—*

But as soon as the doors opened below, the *Quest* felt *horrible* to drive, the joystick bucking left and right like it was possessed. However we normally docked with the *Scout*, I realised, it wasn't standing on end, at the opening of a pipe that was trying to suck the ship up whole.

'*Hatch open*,' the ship's computer said. '*Now lower craft on to scout.*'

'I can't!' I shouted, gripping on like mad to the joystick. 'It's impossible!'

Nobody answered, because nobody else had time *either*. The current grew stronger still, and as the dockerdeckernoctopus *slammed* into our hull, tentacles squeegeeing up the side as it tried desperately to escape the pipe, Stefania put down her binoculars and peered back behind us with dismay.

'Those huge crystal boulders are being sucked back up,' she said. 'There's a massive one coming right behind us!'

'Shoot it then!' I shouted, grappling with the joystick.

'I can't!' she shouted back. 'The guns are on the front, the shot – the shot's impossible!'

'*Lower craft*,' the ship's computer ordered, '*and lift blue lever when successfully docked.*'

188

'Lift ... The blue lever's right in the middle of the docking bay!' Dimi shouted. 'How can I make it? It's impossible!'

That's when it happened – when we just *knew* we couldn't do it.

The ship's speakers crackled to life, a horrible feedback sound that went on and on. First I expected to hear the Erie screaming through them, pleading for help. *Then* I expected to hear Chief Stringer crowing, gloating at our impending doom. But it wasn't either.

It was Our Luke.

'Hello?' Luke said, and me, Stefania and Dimitar all looked at one another. 'Captain ... Captain Ship Driver is that? This is, uh, Spaceman Luke, I think. Can, uh ... can I help with the docking?'

There was a pause.

'Captain *Ship Driver*?' Stefania said. I turned, and all three of us grinned.

'*Spaceman Luke*,' I said. 'Let's get him back.'

With a nod, Stefania swerved the gunner's chair around, so far that the ship's blaster was *nearly* aimed back at us – but not quite. Dimi bent his knees and *leaped*, catching a steel beam that hung from the low ceiling above the middle of the docking bay, before building up a swing

189

back and forth. And I turned back to the control panel, gripping the joystick so hard with one hand, my knuckles cracked and my forearm ached, reaching with the other hand for the ↓ STRAFE button.

Stefania blasted bolt after bolt, which bounced off the rim of the pipe and smashed into the boulder, until it was dust.

I held the ↓ STRAFE, holding the joystick *completely* still with all of my strength, even as I caught a glimpse of Dimi leaping from the metal beam to . . .

CLICK! CLICK!

'Docked!!' Dimi shouted joyfully, hanging from that blue lever with one hand.

'*Docking sequence complete*,' the ship's computer said. And the *Europa Scout* was lifted up into the ship, our friend inside.

'Yes!' I shouted, before I had to strafe further inside the pipe to dodge yet *another* lump of returning rock. Behind me, Stefania and Dimi hefted open the airlock door on Luke's scout ship, and as his excited exclamations came from inside I said it again, just for myself. 'YES.'

'You guys!' Luke – *Our* Luke – said. 'Is it you guys or *Almost-You-Guys*?'

'Us guys!' Stefania shouted with a laugh, and hugged

Luke, the single most emotional thing I've ever seen her do. Dimi was next, slapping Luke's hand into his best bro hug, and they were jumping up and down.

That's when the speakers crackled again.

'Sima,' Chief Stringer said, and there was a *horrible* sneer to his voice. 'Switch on the pump.'

'What?' I said, and pulled the throttle *right* back. 'No. NO!'

It was too late. A BURP echoed down to us, some noise from miles above in the pipe. The *Quest's* thrusters pushed us back to the opening of the pipe, *almost* pushing us out completely. Then, with a lazy, unstoppable power, a wave of water swept upwards, taking the *Quest*, Stacey-the-Erie and every sea creature unlucky enough to be caught in it back up the pipe.

'Sima,' Chief Stringer said. 'Activate the Pulveriser. Set it to *mush*.'

16

Strafe right, strafe left, then BACK!

The *Quest* flew right and left across the metal tunnel, and slowed down slightly. Two giant turtles with fangs and claws spun ahead of us, frantically fighting against the current. But still we kept rising up.

'OK,' I muttered. 'OK – strafe left, up, then pull *BACK*!'

Again I slammed the throttle down. Again the *Quest* slowed down. *PLEASE!* I hoped. A school of krill with red eyes floundered past, *pep-pep-pep*pering the hull.

Still we were sucked up the pipe.

'Navigator Sima,' the Chief said snidely through the speakers. 'Just double-checking – absolutely everything that goes through the Pulveriser is pulverised, correct? To mush?'

'Affirmative, Chief,' Sima said. She didn't sound over-joyed about it . . . but I didn't think this Sima would help us like Officer Sima and Announcer Sima had either.

'Strafe down, then right, then pull *BACK*,' I snarled through gritted teeth, and slammed the throttle back down again. But there was nothing I could do. Our ship – along with loads of scary-but-innocent sea monsters – was being pumped rapidly up the Europa Water Pipe, and no matter what manoeuvre I tried, we couldn't break free from its pull. Not five minutes ago we'd pulled off the *impossible* to save my friend, and now we were going to be turned into mush. And all this was *still* all my fault.

'Ky?' Dimi said.

'I . . .' I began, and pounded the control panel with my fist. 'I don't know what to do.'

There was a long pause.

'You could say hello,' said Luke at last.

Ashamed – *properly* miserable – I turned to face him.

'You tried to steal the money,' he said.

'I know, I—'

'You pushed me out of the car.'

'I didn't—'

'You nearly ran over your *grandma*!'

'Yo, I think I heard that last one wrong,' said Dimi.

'You didn't,' I said miserably. 'You didn't hear wrong. I . . . I thought me and Luke would return to the race, but then, when it turned out we'd gone to another world where we were bank robbers, I . . . I tried to keep the money.'

'You lied to us,' Stefania said disbelievingly. 'You lied to us again. Even after we said it would be unforgivable, you lied to us *again*?!'

'I didn't lie,' I said miserably. 'Not like that. I was just ashamed, so I didn't say the whole truth. I know it's still wrong, but I *knew* you'd find out when we saved him. Just . . . the time to tell you everything before didn't come up. And I . . . I honestly wasn't just taking that money for me, I . . . My mum and dad have to move. We can't afford to rent off Mr Stringer any more.'

'As in, *Chief* Stringer?!' Dimi said, amazed.

I nodded.

'I thought the Infinite Race was just that, a race with a big prize. It seemed like the only way for us to stay round here but . . . but then things went out of control. I just . . . I just didn't want to lose you guys.'

'Why couldn't you just talk to us?' Luke said finally. 'We're your best friends, you can always talk to us.'

I shook my head, out of words, and stared at the ground. Stefania made an exasperated noise, and turned back towards the viewscreen ... when Dimi turned and answered for me.

'He was scared, fam,' he said softly. Luke blinked in surprise. Stef paused, and looked back. 'Our mum worries about money too. Steflon here don't notice, because our mum wants her to concentrate on solving her square puzzles and listening to her square podcasts. But sometimes, Mum has to take things back from the till when we go shopping, and sometimes I catch her crying, and it's ... *la naiba*, I get it. Not being able to live in your home. That's the worst.'

'I ... never thought about it like that,' Luke admitted. 'Not ever. My dad's got money, and I know he means well putting me in all these clubs because Mum's not around and he worries that I get lonely, but my favourite time? It's with you guys. You guys are my family. I've never had to be scared about moving, but I'd be *nuff* scared of you guys moving.'

He walked up to me, looking serious.

'I was really mad at you, Kyan. But you're still my best friend.'

'I really was ready to do anything to save you,' I said.

Luke held out a fist. I bumped it. I bumped Dimi's fist too.

'I guess . . .' Stef said, 'I guess I should've thought about why you did all this, instead of just blaming you.'

She reached out, and bumped my fist.

'Thank you,' I said, but my voice came out a whisper. 'I'm sorry. I'm so sorry for this.' There was a silence that went on and on. Then they all spoke up at once.

'Did I—?'

'I think he just—'

'Ky, did you just say sorry?!'

They started to laugh, they moved in for a hug . . . and then we all stepped back, laughing and cringing about the fact we'd nearly done a group hug.

'YOU ARE GOOD FRIENDS!' Stacey shrieked through the viewscreen, and we all jumped back with a yell.

'Dude, volume control!' Dimi said.

'Stacey!' Stefania exclaimed. 'What are you doing here?'

'I HAVE A PLAN TO DESTROY THIS PIPE COMPLETELY, AND HELP YOUR OTHER SELVES BEFORE THEIR SHIP REACHES THE PULVERISER.'

'Other selves?' I asked. 'How do you know they're our other selves?'

'YOU SOUND THE SAME AS THEM,' Stacey said, and made a kind of shrug, 'AND YOU SOUND DIFFERENT TO THEM. YOU ARE THEIR OTHER

197

SELVES, CORRECT? HOWEVER, MY PLAN MAY NOT
WORK. WE MAY BE TURNED INTO MUSH. IF YOU
CAN GET BACK TO YOUR OWN HOMES, THEN YOU
SHOULD.'

Of course! We *could* leave, now we had Luke. All we
had to do was exit the ship. My eyes strayed to the EJECT
ALL CREW button I'd nearly pressed when I first tried to fly
the *Quest*. Just a quick push, and all our problems would
be over. Only . . .

Only *we'd* done this, hadn't we? *We'd* unblocked this
pipe.

The dockerdeckerplatypus lost its grip on our hull, and
sped off up the pipe, bellowing with fear, and my mind
was made up.

'You guys should go,' I said. 'I . . . don't . . . feel right
leaving the Erie like this. I've caused enough problems for
the people in *our* universe.'

Dimi looked relieved to hear me say that.

'Same here,' he said meaningfully. 'I'm feeling sketchy
as for shooting that blockage out. I wanna help fix
things.'

'I . . . don't feel right about leaving either,' Luke said.
'Other Luke really risked his neck to help the Erie. I don't
know how I ended up in his universe, but if we're supposed

to be a part of our other selves' lives, I want to leave them better, not worse.'

We all nodded at that. I tried not to think of the Kyan and Luke back in Crooklyn, tumbling from that car – although one glance to Luke made me wonder if he wasn't thinking the same thing.

'*And* there's no way I'm missing one last chance to see Jupiter in real life,' Stefania added seriously.

'I swear, your priorities scare me sometimes,' Dimi deadpanned.

Stacey-the-Erie stared through the viewscreen at us all. Then, completely unexpectedly, they punched their arms and legs out straight, that mad mouth stretching wide enough to swallow me whole! It was honestly the scariest smile I think I've ever seen. (But I think it was a smile all the same.)

'THAT IS GOOD TO HEAR,' Stacey said. 'YOUR OTHER LUKE SAID THAT HE HAD FOUND A MAP OF THIS PIPE, IS THAT CORRECT?'

Luke thought for a moment . . . and understanding dawned on his face.

'There's a tablet on the ship, it had all these . . . Just a minute.' He hurried back to the *Scout*, reached through the hatch, and removed another tablet.

'*Syncing screens*,' the ship's computer said. Our viewscreen divided again, showing a blueprint of the pipe on another corner. This showed the opening, deep in an area marked SUBSURFACE OCEAN. The pipe went all the way up through this ocean, and *through* a thin outer layer of the moon marked ICE SHELL. At the very outer edge of the moon was another, bendy pipe marked WATER PUMP. Even as we looked, the red dot showing the *Quest* blinked on to the blueprint. We were halfway up the pipe already!

'I'm guessing that's the Pulveriser at the top,' Dimi said despairingly. I could see why he was scared. Most of the pipe was empty, just two lines to show the walls and nothing else. But the bottom and the top were different. The opening at the bottom had lots of small blaster symbols – all those laser defences that Other Luke had destroyed when he blew that crater in the seabed. The top part of the pipe had even *more* of these symbols all the way through the moon's ice shell. *And*, at the very top, just before the water pump, there were two sets of huge jagged teeth around the pipe.

'Stringer wasn't exaggerating,' I said. 'Those teeth will chomp us up into mush.'

'YES,' Stacey said, 'BUT WHEN WE FIRE A GEYSER,

THE ICY SHELL FREEZES OVER IN SECONDS. IF WE CAN EXPLODE THOSE TEETH, THIS WILL HAPPEN AGAIN, THE SURFACE OF THE MOON WILL FREEZE OVER, AND THE WATER PIPE WILL BE USELESS.'

'That's a great idea!' I said. 'We blow up the teeth, eject from the *Quest*, and get home. How do we destroy it then?'

'WE CANNOT,' Stacey shrieked, 'BUT OUTERSPACEMAN LUKE CAN. I WAS THERE WHEN HIS EXPLOSIONS WENT OFF, AND THEY GREATLY DAMAGED THE PIPE. IF HIS MISSILES CAN MAKE IT PAST THE BLASTERS, THEY MAY BE ABLE TO DESTROY THEM.'

'I'm in,' Luke piped up. 'I went over *all* the controls in the *Scout* when I was trying to get out of there! There's a big button marked FIRE MISSILES!'

(He actually shouted the 'FIRE MISSILES' bit and held his arms out wide. It was good to have him back.)

Stefania looked doubtful though.

'I want to help the Erie,' she said. 'But say if I can shoot down the lasers. And say if Luke can fire the missiles at the right time *and* he destroys the teeth, *and* the water freezes, *and* we fire the ejector seats in time. What about our Other Selves? How is that helping them? They'll be stuck in space, and either they won't be able to breathe or—'

'The Holonetic Helmets!' I interrupted triumphantly. 'They give us an air supply, it said, the first time I used it!'

'*Or*,' Stefania continued, 'they're just floating around ready for Chief Stringer to capture them. How is *that* leaving their lives better?'

That stumped us. But then Stacey piped up.

'WE ERIE HELP OUR FRIENDS. OUR SHIP CAN BE THERE TO COLLECT YOUR OTHER SELVES.'

'How can you tell them to do that from here?' Stefania asked.

Stacey's head tilted back, until it was facing directly up the pipe. Their mouth stretched open, incredibly wide, then suddenly closed, making a strange whistling sound. We all looked somewhere else, a bit awkward. Then Stacey looked back at Stefania.

'IT IS DONE.'

Stefania thought for a moment more, going over all the possibilities in her mind. Finally, she turned to the rest of us and nodded.

'I think it'll work,' she said.

'I AM GRATEFUL FOR YOUR ASSISTANCE,' Stacey said. 'IS IT POSSIBLE FOR US TO BE AS QUICK AS WE CAN? I WOULD LIKE FOR US TO DESTROY THE PUMP BEFORE ANY OF MY SEA FAMILY ARE PULVERISED.'

'OK then, my loud friend,' I said, and looked up at the viewscreen. 'Let's do this. When I push the throttle up we'll boost *quick*. Those lasers aren't that far away now, so Stef, you'll wanna—'

'Ready to fire when necessary!' Stefania barked, sliding into the gunner's chair.

'Right, and Luke, you'll need to be in the scout ship ready to—'

'Missiles are primed and ready!' called Luke from inside the ship.

'Nice one,' I said with a grin.

'What am I supposed to do then?' Dimi demanded. There was an awkward pause.

'Clean the toilets,' Luke and Stefania said from their seats.

'You're all dead to me,' Dimi said, and I couldn't help but laugh.

''K,' I said, and took a deep breath. ''K. Let's do this.'

I pushed up the throttle. The thrusters blasting from the front of the *Quest* stopped, and fired out from the back instead. We jetted forwards, no longer fighting the current but *riding* it, our red dot *racing* up the map of the pipe. I strafed the *Quest* with ease around the doubledeckerplatypus, *pep-pep-pep*pered through the floundering school of red-eyed krill, and barrel-rolled between the long-clawed sea turtles. I was getting better at these controls by the second . . . but then I saw the first laser cannons ahead swivel around to face us.

'Nearly at the first lasers . . .' I began.

PEUNG-PEUNG! Stef fired, and the first two cannons exploded into mini-balls of fire. Still, a hail of energy bolts flew – *CHOON-CHOON-CHOON* – down the pipe towards us, forcing me to swerve out of their way.

'Watch out, Stacey!' I shouted. 'Some bolts are headed down the—'

'Stacey knows,' Dimi said admiringly. Before I could ask what he meant, the megalodon flurried past our side-portals, their long sword dancing like a lightsaber as, with a *FLASH-FLASH-FLASH*, the bolts were bounced back up the pipe, smashing into the laser that had fired them.

'We've got this!' I whooped. 'Bring it on!' But the Chief's voice sounded through the speakers, more smug than ever.

'Navigator Sima, can you confirm that the *Quest* is approaching our top defences?' he said. '*And* the Pulisifier?'

'Confirmed, sir,' Sima said. 'They'll see how hopeless their odds are in three . . . two . . . one . . .'

The smoke from the blasted lasers cleared, and my

heart sank. Ahead of us there must've been *twenty* blasters at least, swivelling on robotic arms to follow our every move. In the distance, beyond the blasters, those gigantic metal teeth of the Pulveriser were snapping shut – *CLANG! CLANG! CLANG!* – again and again and again.

'How can I dodge all those blasters?' I gasped.

'How can I shoot those blasters?' Stefania whispered.

'How can I shoot *past* all those blasters?' Luke groaned.

There was silence, broken only by the echoed *CLANG!* of the Pulveriser getting closer. None of us had an answer. With a desperate sigh, I pulled back the throttle, and we slowed back down, but again, *still* didn't stop, stuck on an elevator to doom. Two more red bolts *zzpped* hopefully towards us, and Stacey rode ahead, batting them back with ease. But the Erie's shoulders were slumped, that amazing mouth pulled down in the biggest, saddest frown I'd ever seen. It was hopeless. We'd done everything, but we just weren't fast enou—

'Fast enough,' I said. '*Fast* enough. We need a *boost*, somehow. We need something to push us through all those blasters all at once, before they can get us.'

Stefania stared blankly at me. Then her eyes widened, and she looked to Dimi.

'*Flush* boost,' she exclaimed. 'Other Luke said something

about a *flush* boost. He said Other Dimi had come up with it.'

'What good is that?' Dimi griped. 'I'm not Other Dimi, am I?'

'Is there no way you can remember it somehow?' I asked. 'No way you're . . . connected somehow?'

Dimi shook his head, frowning.

'I'm not doing anything on here now, am I?' he grumbled. 'I'm not even the Toilet Technician any more . . .'

He paused.

'Dimi?' I asked. 'What is it?'

Dimi shook his head, looking at me, looking *amazed*.

'I don't know if it's my genius idea or *his*, but . . . that sign!'

'What sign?' I said. 'Dimi, what is it?' But he didn't answer me.

'Kyan, speed up,' he said. 'Stefania, take out as *many* of those blasters as you can. Luke, get ready to fire that missile *quick*. Stacey?'

'I CAN HEAR YOU!' the Erie's voice echoed around the ship.

'Bat back as many of those bolts as you can, then try your best to *stop*. This is a job for a Toilet Technician,' he added, and that daft grizzled voice was back again.

Before I could ask him what his idea was, Dimi had disappeared, swinging gracefully down the poles to the back of the ship. He paused, and looked back up at us.

'Go on then!' he chided.

'Yes, Toilet Technician Dimitar,' we all said. And I pushed the throttle up again, speeding forwards. More red bolts *zzpped* for us. I strafed left past them, as Stef spun her chair right and *PEUNG PEUNG* took out one then another. Still the teeth ahead crashed – *CLANG-CLANG-CLANG*. More bolts *zzpped* thicker and faster as more blasters swivelled towards us and fired – *CHOON-CHOON-CHOON*. I dropped low, then – *zzpp* – high; left, then – *CHOON* – right. Stacey rode ahead of us, waving that sword – *FLASH-FLASH* – and sent – *zzpp-zzpp-zzpp* – three bolts hurtling back into another cannon as – *PEUNG-PEUNG* – Stef took out two more behind it and – *zzpp-zzpp-zzpp* – I darted right, left, right, down, and – *FLASH-FLASH* – Stacey ducked back and – *PEUNG* – Stefania missed a shot, and – *zzpp-SMASH* – a bolt slipped through our defence and glanced our hull.

'Dimi!' I called, and my voice was high-pitched with tiredness and terror. The army of blasters was upon us, and the pipe ahead of us was bathed in blood-red laser light. 'Dimi, we've got to—'

'GO!' he roared.

I heard a toilet flush.

There was a second's pause.

I heard *another* toilet flush.

'*Warning,*' the ship's computer said. '*Too much water flushed at once. Uncontrollable acceleration imminent.*'

And we *BOOSTED* up Europa as fast as we'd boosted down it! The blasters all *tried* to shoot us, but they were all too slow, and as we shot between them, they all fired at one another, creating a ball of flame behind us!

'LUKE!' I shouted. 'FIRE, FIRE, FIRE, FI—'

I didn't need to say it. With a *WHOOSH*, the *Scout's* missiles fired out from below, four rockets with wings sliding outwards as they accelerated up, up, *up* . . . into those *CLANG*ing teeth.

'No!' the Chief roared.

BLABLOOOOOM!!!!!

It was the loudest muffled sound I've ever heard. The teeth exploded in a bright, *hot* ball of flame. The ball inflated towards us, and was about to hit us when a wall of water overtook it, knocking our ship back down the pipe with such force that I flew up the ship and slammed into the control panel. Then the wave slowed, pulling us *almost* to a stop, like we'd reached the peak of a pirate ship ride, before we were pulled back upwards, *faster – Faster – FASTER* – towards a circle of white spray that cleared into a circle of black, and stars, and flames . . .

SMASH! We burst out into space! I glimpsed shards of teeth floating by the sidescreens, the Chief's deadly Pulveriser turned to harmless scrap. I turned, and saw Europa's icy shell already freezing over through the rear-view screens behind us, the Chief's greedy straw turned into a powerless tube. But *we* weren't safe yet. A shadow fell across the viewscreen, and I turned to see the Chief's ship glittering menacingly over us. It was the bad ship *Delight*.

'You *traitors!*' the Chief spat through the speakers. 'You destroyed my pipe! SIMA, LOWER THE SHIELDS!'

All at once the twinkling coloured glass that had made the *Delight* seem so good folded back to reveal the cold, grey, *true* steel beneath it. There, in the middle of pipes that belched a luminous, radioactive-looking smoke, was a laser cannon wider and more deadly-looking than any I have ever fired in an online tournament.

'SIMA!' Chief Stringer screamed. 'FIRE THE DEATH RAY!'

'SHIELDS ARE DOWN!' Stacey-the-Erie's voice echoed across the ship. 'I REPEAT, SHIELDS ARE DOWN!'

'Eh?' the Chief said. *Another* shadow loomed towards us; the Erie ship. Those slithering snakes roamed across the wet, spongey ship, but now they were swelling up, inflating from their bellies in a way that, not long ago, I would've found *disgusting*.

'THE ERIE LOOK AFTER THEIR FRIENDS!' Stacey shrieked. And with an almighty *BURP*, those snakes each belched out a huge water bubble! There was a brief, amazed silence, as we watched these shivering balloons of saliva drift slowly past us. And then, suddenly, quietly, the bubbles BURST across the *Delight*'s exposed hull, sending electrical sparks that shuddered and short-circuited their way across it.

'We're hit!' the Chief shrieked. 'Sima, help, WE'VE BEEN HIT!'

'Kyan!' Stefania shouted. 'It's time to go, the Erie are picking us up!'

She was right. The front of the Erie ship opened up again, a gigantic mouth ready to swallow us all whole. With an excited yell I hit the EJECT ALL CREW button, bracing myself for the jetpacks or rocketing chairs, or transporter beams that would hurtle us out of the *Quest*. But instead, the entire floor just opened up with a creak, sending us all tumbling into space with a yell.

'I should've known it'd be a cheap exit,' I moaned. But I didn't really mind. The stars became strings around us and I fell, with a smile, because my friends were falling beside me. Jupiter was to one side, more massive than anything I've ever been able to imagine. The Erie ship was to my other side, the kind of ship that would look murderous and terrifying to anyone who didn't know better. And was it me, or as I floated around to face the bad ship *Delight* for one last time, did I see Navigator Sima staring out from one of the windows at us, her mouth open in shock at these kids who had just defeated her?

'Thanks, Stacey,' I said, and I hope they heard me. 'And sorry. For, y'know . . . humans.'

WHOOMP! We fell into wet leaves, tumbled through twigs and branches, which became thicker and scratchier, until we all SLAPPED into the middle of the biggest one, like it was meant to be. *We're in a tree*, I thought. *But my bedroom doesn't have a tree.*

'Is everyone all right?' said Luke, not sounding all right. 'IS EVERYONE—?'

'Yes!' moaned Dimi and Stefania at once. I saw my bedroom window and groaned.

'Don't panic!' said Luke, panicked. 'We've landed on a *forest planet*. We just need to forage for berries.'

'It's my bedroom, Bear Grylls!' I said. 'We're just the wrong side of the window.'

Luke, Stefania and Dimi clambered on to the branches around me. Stef started to laugh.

'Forage for berries, mate . . .'

'Bear Grylls! HA!'

'Did you see that missile shot? Like, *whoosh*!'

'Slow your roll, Top Gun, you *know* who boosted us to safety . . .'

'Tch, with plumbing. I blew up the pipe! I literally saved a planet!'

'It was a moon, ya goon.'

As Luke and Dimi began to argue about who saved what, Stef nudged me.

'First chance you get, you're going back in, aren't you, Kyan?' she said quietly.

'I don't know . . .' I admitted. 'If I can definitely get back to the world where I'm racing for a million pounds, maybe . . . but then what about the Almost-Kyan in that world? They seem to need money themselves. Then there's the *danger* – I mean, just now we nearly didn't make it, like, *ten times*. Is it really worth it?'

There was a pause. Luke and Dimi had stopped bickering, and finally Luke asked, 'What if you split the money with the other Kyan? Fifty-fifty? Or even . . . even if you just took a bit of the money, a bit you think you earned?'

'If we go back enough times we could all win some,' Stef reasoned. 'We'd soon make enough to help your parents.'

'And together,' said Dimi, 'we could sort out any Chief Stringaling muppet with a beef.'

I looked at them gratefully.

'You'd do that?' I said.

'Explore other dimensions? Er, yeah?' said Stef.

'I think,' Luke said, 'right now I think I could handle anything.'

'One condition,' Dimi said. 'Toilet Technician is on a rota.'

We chuckled, and for a moment just stared contentedly into the night.

'It's night,' said Luke. A look of horror dawned on his face. 'NIGHT! Our parents! We've been gone for hours!'

Shocked, Dimi clambered across to my window and extended a hand to us. Luke was first to go. I was supposed to be next, but Luke was still standing behind the curtains as I climbed in.

'Hurry up!' I whispered. 'Just open the . . .'

I opened the curtains.

213

My dad, Luke's dad and Mrs Anev were in my room, facing away, all stood staring down at the Infinite Race. It had returned back to normal, just an innocent-looking toy track.

'It's crazy,' Dad said. 'Celestine's just got an active imagination.' He was just bending down towards the track when my mum came in on the phone, saw me, and stopped.

'I'm very sorry,' she said into the phone with a *furious* politeness. 'They've just climbed in.'

'It was my fault,' I said.

'Kyan?' my dad muttered, still leaning down towards the track. '*I can hear you!*' He glanced up to the other parents, and finally spotted me. 'Kyan!' he said, and jerked up, tripping back in his big, stompy, clodhopping safety boots, with the steel toe caps and hard, crushing soles. STOMP went one boot, STOMP went the other, and there was a horrible snapping sound with every step.

The Infinite Race, the only way I could think of to save our home, was smashed to bits.

17

'So what have you got to say for yourself?' Mum said, as Mrs Anev's shouting receded down the street. Dad stood next to her looking like he wished we were back in the days when dads weren't just *allowed* to hang their naughty kids up by their thumbs but were *expected* to. I stared dejectedly at the broken pieces of the Infinite Race, and had no answers.

'Just . . . wanted . . .' I muttered, trying to think of something to say. 'Our flat.'

This would be it. The Big Tell-Off. Blood, mud and fireworks, with two parents combining forces into some *nuclear* destruction. But instead, Mum blinked. Dad's head dropped, and he put a hand on her arm.

'You want me to . . . ?' he began, but Mum shook her head.

'Let me.'

Dad nodded, kissed her, and patted my shoulder on his way out. Mum stared at me again.

'You know what's been happening with Mr Stringer,' she said at last, so tired that I *wanted* the shouting. 'We should've talked about it with you. I'm sorry, we just didn't have time. Didn't make time. But Kyan . . . *you scared us.* Your dad's been shouting your name all round the park. Your sister said you'd disappeared into some toy!'

'She *told*,' I said bitterly to myself.

'She told a fib to keep you out of trouble for leaving

without telling us,' Mum said sharply. 'OK, so maybe her stories could do with some work – I don't know how she thought *anyone* but your dad would seriously think you'd gone into a toy racetrack – but she was looking out for you.'

'I really don't want to move,' I murmured. 'Will we have to?' I looked up and saw tears in Mum's eyes. *Please don't cry*, I thought.

'We're working every hour we can to avoid that,' Mum said. 'But I . . . I can't promise, Kyan, I just can't. I am *so* sorry about that. *So* sorry.'

She gripped my arm and squeezed it. After a moment she wiped her eyes, quickly, like she was annoyed to have to do it, and forced a smile.

'Now, even though we can't afford Football Factory, that doesn't mean you'll have a summer without any clubs at all. Dad looked in the Community Centre for ones we can afford, and there's a few options I thought might be OK.'

Mum hurried out of the room, and returned with some fliers in her hand. They weren't promising; spelling mistakes in the titles, stretched-out photos where the kids looked impossibly tall and thin on one page, and stretched wide like mutant frogs on the next.

'Flag Waving Club,' I said doubtfully. 'Is that even a thing? *Handwriting* Club? Cipher Club, *Budgeting* Club, Li— *Litterpicking* Club! Even this Flower Fun Club just looks like we're tidying up that man's garden for him . . .'

Then I caught a concerned look on Mum's face. My parents needed me at a club while they're at work, I realised. It was now the only way I could help save the flat. And as bitter as that thought was, I forced a smile.

'They all look so *good*!' I said, squeezing that last word out. 'Can I pick one in the morning?'

Mum considered this. 'Actually it's too late to call any of them now, so as long as you're up early, then yeah. We *will* talk about your disappearing act tomorrow too, but it's time to sleep now, OK?'

'Goodnight, Mum. Sorry for making you worried.'

Mum hugged me tightly.

'Goodnight, Ky. Get to sleep.'

She left, and I went to sleep like she asked.

Course I didn't! I *had* to see if the Infinite Race would work. As soon as I heard the TV come on, I jumped out of bed, and pieced all of the broken pieces of track together. It wasn't promising; most of the pieces were snapped and bent into sharp shards, and none of the clicky bits would click together. Still, I *had* to try. With the track lying loosely along the floor, I grabbed the first toy car I found, shuffled like mad across the rug, pushed the car forwards to the end of the broken track, pulled it back and . . .

'DON'T go out again, Kyan!' said Celestine from the hallway. I'd stupidly, *stupidly* forgotten to shut the bedroom door!

The TV sounds paused, and Mum's footsteps paced back around.

'ARE YOU ACTUALLY SERIOUS?!' Mum shouted. 'SERIOUSLY SERIOUS?! YOU LEFT THE HOUSE WITH YOUR FRIENDS WITHOUT TELLING US! YOU ARE IN *BED* NOW, AND EXCEPT FOR WHATEVER CLUB YOU CHOOSE, YOU ARE *GROUNDED* WITH *NO* SCREEN! *DON'T* WORRY ABOUT BEING BORED AFTER CLUB EITHER – THERE IS A *LONG* LIST OF CHORES!'

With one last *fierce* smile, Mum went back to the telly and I stood there, swaying like a hurricane had hit. That's when I saw Celestine looking nervously out at me from her doorway.

'Do you even know what the Infinite Race was?' I hissed. 'It was the thing that could've saved us from having to move. But you're a *snitch*! You lost us our *home*! We would be *much* happier without you here.'

I regretted the words as soon as they came out of my mouth. A look of the *worst* hurt crashed across Celestine's face, and she ducked back into her room. I was left standing in the dark. Worst of all, when I looked down at the Infinite Race, there were no sparks, nothing. It was nothing more than a broken toy.

After a night of amazing dreams, about big-money races and intergalactic smackdowns of water-stealing villains, I woke up with a flier for Flag Waving Club in my hand . . . and then felt *proper* sorry for myself. Those dreams were smashed to pieces on the floor now, just a pile of broken titanium or terrarium or whatever that stupid code had said in the stupid . . .

The Rules!

I hadn't checked the Infinite Race Instructions since we'd returned from Europa Moon the night before. But after every mission my Level had gone up and a new message had appeared like magic on the Instruction Manual. Was there *any* chance that there might be one telling me how to get a new racetrack and save our home?

I fell out of bed, muscles aching – underwater space battles were *tiring*, I realised – and stumbled to the broken racetrack. The Instruction Manual was still where I'd left it, on the floor next to the track. When I caught a glimpse of those golden letters, I snatched it up with excitement.

Prepare for the Ride of Your Lives

Congratulations on completing your third mission! But fix up and look sharp. You are not yet at Level 3.

Level 3 Infinity Racers who don't look after their things must display a range of skills, including a higher standard of code-breaking. With this in mind, be sure to remember Key Word Codes, Rotacar Racevator, Racevator Rotacar, and Qb abg or fb pyhzfm ntnva. Abg jvgu lbhe genafcbeg. Abg jvgu lbhe genafcbeg'f genafcbeg. Naq arire jvgu gur enprgenpx.

ANOTHER code?! I groaned. But the message about

things needing to 'fix up and look sharp' gave me a glimmer of hope. Did that mean what I wanted it to mean, that my track would be fixed if I solved the code? There was only one way to find out.

Frantically I copied out the code into my notebook. But how to solve it? There weren't any numbers, like there had been when Grandma had been helping me. At first the bit about 'Racecar Rotavator' got me excited that it was something more about things being backwards . . . but then I realised that *this* code didn't actually say 'Racecar Rotavator', but 'Rotacar Racevator' . . . which didn't make any sense at all. Also it said that I had to know about 'Key Word Codes'. But what were they?

I needed help. Stefania might be able to work it out, but then I remembered that my friends were all starting Football Factory that day. That made my spirits sink even *lower.*

'Come on,' I said out loud, determined not to give up. Surely there was *somebody* who could help, although it would also have to be after these stupid clubs, unless . . .

Unless . . .

With a sudden excitement, I went back to the pile of holiday club pamphlets Mum had given me. After Flag Waving, and Litterpicking, there it was:

CIPHER CLUB

WITH EDIE SCRAP

ABBOTS BROMLEY SCHOOL. RECEPTION CLASSROOM
9 A.M. TOMORROW.

LISTEN
SOLVE CODES
DON'T EXPECT A SLAP ON THE BACK.

FREE

'Sorry, Mum,' I blurted out. 'Can I go to Cipher Club?'

Mum was hurrying around the kitchen getting our packed lunches ready. She stopped and looked at me in surprise.

'You sure?!' said Mum. 'That one was posted through our door yesterday, but this Edie Scrap doesn't seem too welcoming. I'd thought of sending you as punishment. Who's expecting a slap on the back?!'

'I know,' I said with a grin – although that line had made me even *more* excited to go. *Slap on the back . . . backslaps to be slapped back* ... Could this Edie woman have anything to do with Infinity Racing? 'Still, it looks really interesting though.'

'OK!' Mum said. Secretly I could tell she was relieved that I'd picked the one club marked 'FREE'. 'I'll let your Dad know.'

'Can I use your phone to GroupMe Luke and Stef and Dimi first?' I asked. Her lips pursed, about to form the words *You're grounded*, so I added quickly, 'I just wanted to wish them luck at Football Factory.'

Yeah, it was a guilt trip, reminding her that all my friends were there and I wouldn't be. Yeah, I felt bad when Mum's face did this mini-crumpling thing. But I sent the messages anyway.

> enjoy FF 🏟️ 🏟️ 🏟️ 🏟️ but i found new rule for Infinite Race

> not Level 3 yet but NEARLY if i solve a code 😖 😸 😟

> might get us new track 🏁

> so going cipher club 🧠

> it's at school reception classroom 😯

> the advert sounds like they kno about infinity races 😈

224

Hmm. I'll admit it – as soon as I finished that last message I realised two things. First, my emoji game goes *way* down when I'm not thinking straight. Second, there was so much in those messages that might be completely foolish. Why *would* solving the Instructions code fix the racetrack? It was probably a code for an Infinity Racer who *hadn't* let their track get smashed up. And so what if the pamphlet mentioned 'a slap on the back'? What if Edie Scrap was just a very, *very* unfriendly person?

Those niggling questions kept coming as my mum dropped me off at the school gates – and soon a severe case of the uneasies settled on my spine. I'm going into Year 6, so *basically* I'm king o' the school. But just yesterday I had been dropped into a monster's nest, and now, the further I walked through those empty, echoing corridors, the creepier they seemed – and the stranger this Cipher Club clearly was. Even by the standards of all the other dodgy kids' clubs, the flier had been basic. Where was everybody else now? What if Edie Scrap wasn't anything to do with the Infinite Race at all? What if she couldn't even help me with this code? What if . . .

What if she was an axe murderer?

By the time I reached the Reception class, all my senses were on edge. I heard voices coming from inside the classroom; hushed, suspicious voices, the kind that axe murderers use, probably. I paused outside the door . . . and the voices paused too.

OK, I thought, *OK, this is it. One, two . . .*

'Three!' a familiar voice shouted, and the door *pulled* open, sending me sprawling inside.

'Kyan!' Luke shouted, and I looked up to see my friends standing over me, holding stationery-like weapons. 'You *haven't* been murdered!'

'I . . .' I said, completely and utterly shocked. 'I . . . What are you doing here?!'

'We didn't want to leave you to solve the code by yourself,' Stefania explained. 'So we snuck out of Football Factory and came to help you.'

'You left . . . You can't leave Football Factory!' I exclaimed. 'You've been looking forward to it for ages!'

'It's fine,' Dimi said. 'It's cool. We were just getting striking tips off the top scorers in the Premier League . . .'

Dimi's voice cracked with grief, and he trailed off, facing away slightly. I really felt for him, *really* appreciated this. But Stefania rolled her eyes.

'He'll be *fine*,' she said. 'We'll go back tomorrow. But this coding club is *dead*, Ky. Where's the teacher? Where's the other kids? Luke was getting all freaked out.'

'Just Luke, yeah?' I said with a grin, looking at the stapler in her hand. Stefania put it down, reddening. But I wasn't going to tease her any more. My friends being here right now was the best thing ever.

'I wasn't fazed for a *second*, cuz,' Dimi said. 'You said the advert mentioned Infinity Racing, right? It promised you a new racetrack, didn't it? This club's probably just for us!'

'Yes!' I said. I was reassured at first – I hadn't thought of that possibility. But then the rest of what he'd said sunk in. 'Although – well ... I mean ... the flier didn't *exactly* mention it. It said ... I mean ... it didn't promise a new racetrack either ... and neither did the code ... But – *but* ... But ... the flier *did* say "Don't expect a slap on the back". Eh? You know? Like the clue in the Instructions, "Backslaps to be slapped back"!'

Well, if I already had doubts about this club being of any help, the looks on my friends' faces then made me feel even worse. Luke did his kind, encouraging smile, like he always does when I'm chatting rubbish. Stefania frowned, like I needed a slap across the head for such a stupid idea. And Dimi turned away again.

'Premier League,' he mumbled. I *swear* he brushed away a tear. 'Premier League footballers coaching us, and we leave it for "Don't expect a slap on the back".'

Just when things couldn't get any worse, I felt something move in the doorway. I turned, and found myself face to face with ... a strange, mangled-looking balloon animal.

''Rrrr'ey up, Rrrrryan Grrreen!' the balloon animal said. 'Rrrrorry too keep roo rrraiting! Rrrr'I needed the rrroilet! I'm Edie Scrrrrrrap!'

I was so stunned, I didn't say a word. Then a woman's face poked out smiling from the door. When she saw me, her face dropped.

'Wait, you're *old*!' she said. 'How come this is in Reception then?'

Edie Scrap was a pale-skinned whirlwind, with short, spiky hair, punk rock clothing, a massive jumbly handbag, and a smiley face that was always *slightly* confused. She looked about my mum's age, but Mum reckons I say that with anybody younger than Grandma and older than me. She held out her hand, and as she took in my stunned face, her smile faltered.

'You *are* Kyan, aren't you?' she said. 'Your dad rang up this morning to double-check this club was free? Said something about In-App Purchases?'

'... That sounds like him,' I said finally.

'He also said you like balloon animals too, but to be fair, he sounded like it was a weird question.' Edie smiled apologetically. 'Sorry, duckie – I was only offered this job yesterday. To be honest, it came as a bit of a surprise, being as I'm a mechanic. Still, we'd better get started, seeing as I'm late. Phew, takeaway night'll be the death of me.'

'Eww,' Stefania said, and Edie blinked, as if only seeing my friends standing beside me now. Fortunately, she seemed as nice as she was doolally. It was completely different to how the Cipher Club advert had made her sound, I realised.

'Do you guys all wanna learn about coding too then? Mega! Hey, maybe they'll have me back next year. I could do with the money right enough, eh?'

My friends stared, not quite sure if that was actually a question.

'Mega!' Edie repeated anyway. 'Now take a seat and we'll get started – they've given me a blinding puzzle for us to solve. Even I don't know the answer, but never you fear – I love a good code, me. Lucky coincidence when you think about it!'

As she walked to the whiteboard – tripping on the side of the teacher's desk, her massive bag swinging around and sweeping a pot of pens across the floor – I sighed, feeling a heavy disappointment. There was surely *no way* this club and its mad teacher could have anything to do with the Infinite Race. Had I been too hopeful with the Instructions as well? Did 'fix up and look sharp' even mean that the track would be repaired, or was it something else, something that I would *never* find out because I didn't have a track any more? Still, as we took a seat, Stefania nudged me.

'You might as well ask her about the code while we're here,' she whispered.

I nodded, and took out the Instructions.

'Er, actually I brought my own code to solve . . .' I began. But it was too late.

'*Codes*,' Edie whispered, and leaped around, 'are *super-special secrets!*' She covered her eyes with her hands and peered through them like she was about to play peekaboo. I stared back, utterly flabbergasted, until finally she took her hands away from her eyes.

'Sorry,' she said awkwardly. 'I really did think you'd be four when I planned this. Let's find something more suitable for you, eh?'

'If I was four I would be *so* scared right now,' Dimi murmured, as Edie cheerfully opened her massive handbag and took out all kinds of random things – her

mangled balloon animal, a blowtorch, some blue triangle sunglasses and a wrench. Finally, she took out a sheaf of A4 paper, and flipped through them, muttering to herself.

'Let's leave out "Story Time". Leave out the "I Can Spell my Name" game. The coding song? Nope, lose that . . .'

'Yeah, so I did actually bring in my own—' I began again.

'Ah!' Edie exclaimed. 'The code!' With the papers in hand, she took out a marker pen and hurried back to the whiteboard. As she scrawled and scribbled across it, I stared glumly down at my code. I would just have to try to solve it with my friends.

'Stef,' I whispered. 'Will *you* look at this? I only came to this stupid club to solve it.'

Stefania took the Instructions off me, studying the new golden letters. Then she froze.

'Oh my days,' she murmured, and looked up at the board. 'Oh my *days*!'

'What?'

'*You* were right, Kyan. She's got something to do with the Infinite Race.'

I followed her gaze to the whiteboard. And for one second I couldn't breathe. The code – that code that had magically appeared in the Instructions? The code I had dared to hope might help me fix the racetrack if I could solve it?

Edie Scrap had written that code on the whiteboard.

18

Be sure to remember Key Word Codes, Rotacar Racevator, Racevator Rotacar, and Qb abg or fb pyhzfm ntnva. Abg jvgu lbhe genafcbeg. Abg jvgu lbhe genafcbeg'f genafcbeg. Naq arire jvgu gur enprgenpx.

'Right,' said Edie. '*Right.* For thousands of years, people have hidden information behind *ciphers*, special secret ways of writing that hide the message from spies and enemies. Can any of you *senior citizens* think of a famous cipher, a famous code?'

'Morse code,' Luke said. He and Dimi were still unaware that our coding teacher had written out *my* code on the board.

'Good,' said Edie. Suddenly she clapped her hands and tapped her feet in a strange, fast-slow rhythm. 'G! O! O! UDD!'

'Is that really Morse code?' Luke asked.

'Good question!' Edie said cheerfully. 'Morse code was invented by Samuel Morse, an inventor who wanted to send instant messages by tapping out dots and dashes across telegraph lines, long before texts or *even* emails. Any more?'

'You . . . you didn't answer my question . . .' Luke began.

'Keyword codes!' I shouted, and studied Edie's face for any sign that she was somehow leading me back to the Infinite Race. But there was no reaction I could spot.

'Hmm,' she said. 'That's an interesting idea, duckie. It is in the clue. Do you know much about keyword codes then?'

'I don't know,' I said suspiciously. 'Do I?'

'. . . I don't know,' Edie said. 'Do you?'

'I don't know,' I snapped. 'Do I?'

'I don't know, Ky,' Dimi muttered, with a strange look to me. 'Do you?'

'. . . Tell you what,' Edie said, looking slightly freaked out. 'Why don't we learn a bit about keyword codes, and we can see if Kyan's suggestion was right?'

She turned to the board, and began to scribble

something else beneath the code. As she did, Dimi leaned over and nudged me on the arm.

'Bruv,' he said. 'What's going on? She's going to run away if you don't stop. Cool, yeah? Mişto.'

'I *am* mişto,' I said huffily. 'I just want to solve this stupid code!' I must've been a bit loud, because Edie glanced back with alarm, and her writing started to fall down the board, like Celestine's does when there aren't lines on the page. When she turned back to correct it, I showed Dimi the Instructions.

'It's the same code,' I whispered. 'She's written the *same code*.'

When she'd finished, Edie turned and blinked – maybe because now me, Stef *and* Dimi stared back at her with narrowed eyes and suspicious glares. But then I looked past her to the board, and my interest grew. She'd drawn a grid with two rows, showing all the letters of the alphabet from A to Z on the bottom, and blank spaces above it.

A	B	C	D	E	F	G	H	I	J

'Keyword codes,' Edie said, 'are codes where the alphabet

is changed by a special password. They're *really* simple to do, but they can *only* be solved if we have that word. All we have to do is enter the keyword into the top line, and that gives us our *cipher* – our new alphabet.'

'Rotacar Racevator!' Stefania said suddenly. 'Of course! We just need to start the alphabet with Rotacar Racevator and it'll give us the code!'

'I hope so!' said Edie cheerfully.

'But do you *know* so?' I hissed, and again she glanced with alarm back at me.

'Ky!' Luke said, when she turned back to face the board. 'Why are you being so rude?!'

'That code!' I whispered. 'That's *our* code! The one on the Instructions!'

I gestured to Stefania, who had flipped the Instructions over, and was scribbling this possible solution furiously on the back.

'That's amazing!' said Luke. 'What's the odds of . . . *oh* . . .' And as Edie finished her grid and turned around, she was faced by me, Luke and Dimi, all staring suspiciously at her.

R	O	T	C	A	E	V	B	D	F
A	B	C	D	E	F	G	H	I	J

'You've missed loads of the letters,' I objected.

'Of course I haven't, brains,' Stefania snapped, still completing her grid. 'I didn't want to *repeat* the letters.'

'That's right!' Edie said. 'Although let's keep this a Positivity Corner! In this keyword code, we change "A" for "R", "B" for "O", "C" for "T", and so on. We don't want to repeat letters, or the cipher won't work. Having said that, the fact that there are so many repeating letters in "Rotacar Racevator" makes me wonder if this is in fact a keyword code after all. Good idea anyway, Kya—'

'Dammit!' Stefania said, and pounded the table. 'She's right. It doesn't work.'

'Well, let's not have a mardy,' Edie said, looking *alarmed* now. 'This is just a fun club ...' But I wasn't listening. Stefania showed me what she'd written, swapping the letters around according to her cipher:

Qb abg or fb
MH EHK BA

'What a waste of time,' I sighed, and rubbed my head. 'All right. What other keywords might it be?'

'That's an interesting suggestion,' Edie said. 'But the difficulty in solving keyword codes is that unless you *know* the keyword, it really could be—'

'Infinite Race!' Luke exclaimed.

'Eh?' Edie said. 'No, what I mean is that we're not helping ourselves by just trying to guess—'

'It *still* doesn't work,' Stefania said, and SLAMMED the table again. 'Come on, people! THINK! THINK! What's the keyword?'

'Infinity!' I shouted.

'Race!' Dimi shouted.

'Do you ever think your parents are pushing you too hard?' Edie said weakly.

'No!' Luke roared, and got to his feet, shocking all of us. 'NO! We want to know what this code means and we want to know now! No more lies, Edie! We need ANSWERS!'

There was a moment's pause. We'd all gone too far. Luke sat back down, looking horrified at what he'd done. And as I looked up at Edie's unhappy face, I suddenly realised something very important.

'I . . .' Edie said. 'I'm really, *really sorry*, but I think you kids've got the wrong end of the stick. Maybe . . . maybe me doing this wasn't such a good idea.'

'You don't know anything about the Infinite Race at all,' I said.

'What?' Edie said, her voice pleading. 'What's the

Infinite Race? I told you, I'm a mechanic. I just happen to like codes – honest!'

Edie paused, and shook her head, picking up the eraser and rubbing at the whiteboard with such a sad expression on her face that I felt bad for her.

'I knew this job was too good to be true,' Edie mumbled to herself. 'Just thought it'd be exciting to teach you kids ciphers like *I'm* into 'em.'

'Miss . . .' I began, but she was concentrating on the board.

'*Look at me, I'm the codemaster*,' she continued. 'Tch, *idiot*! I shoulda stuck to the spanners and sockets.'

'*Say something*,' I urged the others. Stefania nodded, and put up her hand.

'I think you've used permanent marker,' she said.

'*Stef*,' Dimi said, and shook his head.

'What?'

'That's not exactly what I meant by saying something,' I admitted. Luckily, Luke raised a trembling hand, his best angel face on tight.

'I am *really* sorry, miss,' he said. 'We just really enjoy your class.'

'You don't have to humour me,' Edie said. 'I know I'm not cut out to control a classroom.'

'You are!' I exclaimed. 'Honest! Look at us – if anything, you've got us *too* excited about codes!'

Edie stopped trying to rub off the permanent marker. She turned and peered suspiciously over her shoulder at us.

'Serious?' she said at last.

'*Honest*,' I repeated.

'Promise?'

'Promise,' Luke said sincerely.

There was a pause . . . then Edie *launched* the whiteboard around to a clean side, and began to scribble frantically.

'MEGA!' she said. 'I LOVE codes.'

'I think that's *still* permanent marker, miss . . .' Luke offered, but she was too excited to care.

'A good code is like a painting or a book or a puzzle,' she continued. 'The more clues you get, the more little clues you get to the person who made it up. And you know what? The *minute* I twigged that this weren't any straight-forward keyword, I sorta *got* the person who made this code up. It was weird, I tell ya – almost like I knew 'em somehow!'

She paused and looked to see if we were paying atten-tion. We were all listening intently. 'Now,' she went on, and turned away from the board. 'We have this clue, and nothing else. It drops a hint that there's a keyword clue in there – that *wasn't* a bad guess, Kyan – but then there's summat a mite tricksy going off. It's almost like the person *wanted* us to take a dodgy turn, and end up racing the wrong way down a one-way street, like as happened to me twice on the drive down here. So if keywords aren't the answer, what *else* do we have as a possible clue?'

We all stared at the clue, written out on the whiteboard again:

Be sure to remember Key Word Codes, Rotacar Racevator, Racevator Rotacar, and Qb abg or fb pyhzfm ntnva. Abg jvgu lbhe genafcbeg. Abg jvgu lbhe genafcbeg'f genafcbeg. Naq arire jvgu gur enprgenpx.

'. . . Rotacar Racevator?' Stefania said slowly.

'Very good,' Edie said.

'But those words aren't right,' Luke objected, and Edie nodded with a smile.

'Good shout, Luke, there,' she said. 'What *should* they be?'

'Racecar Rotavator,' I said instantly.

'That is . . . absolutely right! Wow, you're quick! "Racecar Rotavator" *are* real words. Now, what *else* is interesting about "Racecar Rotavator"? It probably *seems* like nothing, but—'

'It's a palindrome,' Stef said. 'They spell the same backwards as well as forwards.'

Edie stared. 'How old did you say you kids were?' she said.

But then it suddenly hit me.

'Wait . . . *Backwards!* I exclaimed. 'It's *backwards*! If we—'

'Turn the alphabet backwards!' Dimi piped up. 'That's the clue, innit!'

Straight away we all began to scribble away at our notebooks while Edie watched with a smile. I had two whole letters written down before Stef threw her pen down in exasperation.

'It doesn't work,' she said.

'It ain't "Racecar Rotavator" though, is it?' Dimi said. 'It's . . . Potatovator Toetatovator or whatever.'

'*Well, fancy that!*' Edie said. 'That's not *quite* a palindrome, is it?'

Rotacar – Racevator
Racecar – Rotavator

'What's that then?' Edie asked. 'It's bloody clever, that's what.'

242

'It . . .' I began, and stared, trying to make my mind click out of place like it had when I'd worked out the original Instructions. 'It's . . . sort of . . . *half* . . . backwards.'

We sat there in dumb silence for a long second. Then, suddenly, Stefania made this *whooshing* breath she makes when she gets a *great* idea.

Edie grinned, looking delighted.

'I'll let you write it out, duck, since you're the quick one.'

Furiously Stefania began to scribble on her notepad, and we all got up, rushing to gather around her desk as she wrote. Like I had been doing with the keycodes, she started to write the alphabet on the top . . . only this time she stopped at 'K' and whispered a sum.

'Twenty-six letters in the alphabet, so thirteen letters each, *a-b-c-d-e-f-g-h-i-j-k-l-m* . . . M.'

'That's the one,' Edie said quietly, still smiling. Stefania carried on writing, all the way up to 'M', before writing the other letters beneath it. Like this:

A	B	C	D	E	F	G	H	I	J	K	L	M
N	O	P	Q	R	S	T	U	V	W	X	Y	Z

'So . . .' Stefania said, and looked up to Edie for confirmation. 'Every "A" is an "N", every . . .'

'. . . "B" is an "O",' Edie said with a grin. 'And "C" is a "P", and so on.'

'Mega!' Dimi exclaimed, and Edie's grin got even wider. 'So, in this clue, the first letter is a "Q"—'

'Which should be a "D",' I said, craning over Stefania's shoulder.

'"B" next,' Luke said. 'So that's an "O".'

'Then "A" is "N" – no, *space* first!' I said, and as we all started to shout out letters, Stefania raced ahead, scribbling furiously.

'Do . . . not . . . be . . . so . . .'

At last Stef finished. She sat back, smiling, and I read the deciphered rule aloud . . .

'*Do not be so clumsy again. Not with your transport. Not with your transport's transport. And never with the racetrack.*'

We sat there in a stunned silence.

'Huh,' Edie said. 'That's a strange message. Back in my day they just used to ask you to join the Babysitters' Club.'

'I can't believe it,' I said. 'It worked. It *worked*!'

'*Did* it work?' Stefania asked.

'We've gotta go see!' I exclaimed, and we all shot up, scraping our chairs out.

'Wait . . . What?' Edie said.

'Thank you so much,' I said, 'but it's time to go.'

'. . . Oh,' Edie said, her face falling. 'Yeah. I suppose one code's enough, in't it. Just make sure you let your parents know you're leaving, won't ya? They'll want to be finding another club for you the rest of this week.'

We all stopped, bags hanging half on our shoulders, and looked at Edie. She was disappointed, I could see. Gutted, even. She'd helped us after I'd been rude to her. Thanks to her, I might even have another chance with the Infinite Race. But *ohhh*, I really wanted to go and find out now.

'I think we have to stay, bro,' Dimi said quietly. 'It's like when I left Football Factory, innit? It *hurts*, but it's the right thing to do.'

I thought about this. And I nodded, sitting back down.

'Actually, miss, what other codes do you know about?' I asked.

Edie Scrap *was* a good teacher, even if she was a bit bonkers. And because we wanted her to feel like a good teacher, we all joined in with every activity – even her coding song, 'Should I Stay or Should I Code?', which was *way* more fun and involved *way* more screaming than the usual songs I've heard for four-year-olds. She also taught us about other types of codes that she was into. We did Pig

Latin – *erfectpay otay oolfay eacherstay*. We learned about Capoeira, a dance that enslaved people would sometimes use to send messages long ago in Brazil. We even coded our own names into anagrams – just call me *Eek Granny*.

But all day, the Infinite Race was on my mind, and after the club had finished we couldn't sprint out to the car park fast enough. It was empty, except for a gleaming red sports car and my grandma's old hatchback.

'So how was it?' my grandma said, then, 'Oh!' as I got into the front, Stef and Dimi squeezed into the back, and Luke piled into the hatchback seat of her old car. 'You all went to the Cipher Club?'

'It was amazing,' I said. 'When I told the others about it, they left Football Factory and came to join me!'

'Right,' Grandma said, eyeing the others in the back with suspicion. 'I'm sure their parents will be over the moon after spending all that money on the football.'

'Oh,' Stef said hurriedly, 'we'll be back there tomorrow. Mum told us just to go here today, to try it.'

'But she didn't want to *know* what we did,' Dimi said. 'So don't tell her.'

'Shh!' Stefania said, and tutted. 'I swear you're so obvious!' As they began to bicker furiously, Grandma pulled her car forwards, and we passed the red sports car. It had loads of mods all over it – a beefy, low-down bumper, glimmering alloys that turned gently in the wind, and a sharp spoiler at the back that made it look like a home-made rally car.

'Very snazzy,' Grandma said. 'He likes fixing up motors, I see, your teacher.'

'She ...' I said. 'She's a mechanic normally, although she didn't say she'd done *that* to her car, it's well cool. Although...'

It was strange. As we pulled away, the sunlight glinted off Edie Scrap's car roof so brightly that I couldn't make it out. Without a roof, that car looked strangely familiar.

'Huh...' I said, thinking.

Edie walked up to it, gave us a wave, and got in, putting on a pair of sunglasses.

'*Blue* sunglasses,' I whispered. 'It can't be!' Quickly I wrote out 'E D I E S C R A P' in my notepad. There was an 'S', I saw. There was a 'P'. There was an 'I', a 'D', an 'E', an 'R' ...

'Just a sec,' I said, and opened the car door.

'Kyan? Kyan!' Grandma shouted, and braked hard. I was already racing across the car park.

*   *   *

'Edie?' I said, approaching the car door. 'Edie Scrap?'

The car's engine fired up, and the window rolled down, but the sun was in my eyes and I couldn't see Edie properly. I walked closer, until the car blocked the sun, and . . . I gasped.

Edie had *changed*. She sat straighter. Her messy hair was tidied into a quiff, and the eyes behind her sunglasses were hard, her scowl was *mean*. She rested one arm on the window, and looked out at me.

'Edie Scrap. Spider Ace,' I said. 'You're *Spider Ace*! You were in the first race!'

'Huh,' said Spider Ace. 'Took you long enough to figure it out.'

'So you *did* know about the Infinite Race!' I said.

'*I* do. Edie Scrap dun't even know I share her strings from time to time.' Spider Ace's scowl deepened, and she jabbed a finger at me. 'Now you listen to me, Sulky Pants,' she said. 'I've gorra lot of miles to travel, and norra lorra seconds to waste. If you want to ask a question, it best be a whole lot more interesting than *Who be thee?*'

I stared at her, a million questions running through my mind. What was the Infinite Race for? Why did *I* have it? How could I save our home? But there was one question that kept returning, the one that I knew would bother me *forever* if I didn't find the answer.

'The other Kyan . . .' I said. 'The Kyan and Luke we left in Crooklyn. Are they . . . ?'

'The famous Bank Blag Boys of Dimension 367, Ky-Ky Mo' Green and Lil' Luke, are now in hospital having survived a death-defying leap across the Crooklyn Bridge,' she said, and gave me a curt nod. 'Good question.'

'I ruined their lives,' I said.

'Don't be so daft. You saved their lives!' Spider barked, like she was telling me I'd left the toilet seat up. 'They'll get a shorter sentence because they're kids, and more importantly, Officer Stringer is in prison. Had you not stepped in, it's certain he wouldn't be, and very likely that things would've gone much, much worse. Not that you didn't risk it all, fighting over money like you did.'

'You saw that,' I said, shame flushing my face.

'Why d'you think I set you up with a follow-on rescue mission?'

'Wait,' Luke said. I turned around, to see my friends all standing, horrified, behind me. '*You* sent me to Europa?!'

'Why?' Stefania said. 'Some kind of stupid test or what?!'

Spider Ace raised her eyebrows.

'You think you're ready to know all that? I don't. You've still got to prove yourselves in my eyes.'

'How?' I asked.

'Keep doing what you're doing,' Spider Ace said. 'Make your other lives better. Don't be dorks, and don't be villains.' Then she looked past me and my friends, and revved up the engine, a deep, phlegmy snarl that sounded like a lion with a frog in its throat.

'And. *Beat. Mr. Stringer,*' she said.

And then, in a cloud of dust, Spider Ace drove off.

19

'You're quiet,' Grandma said, as we drove home. My mind was whirling, not just with Spider Ace and the Infinite Race, but all of the crazy things I had seen over the past two days.

'Just tired,' I said. 'That coding club was good but it was hard work.'

Grandma took this in, nodding slightly.

'Your sister was asking after you too,' she said after a pause. 'I caught her in your bedroom.'

'In my room?' I said. 'She's not supposed to . . . Why was she there?!'

'Calm down,' Grandma said. 'She wasn't prying. She was writing you a sorry letter, if you must know. She was just leaning on one of your game boxes to write it.'

I wracked my brains to see how I could be annoyed about this. Even more annoyingly, I couldn't think of anything.

'Hmph,' I said. 'She best not have taken anything.'

Grandma sighed, and gave me a look.

'OK,' she said after a moment. '*I* have a code for you. Well, not quite a code. A, uh, riddle, let's say.'

'What's the reward for solving it?'

'The answer,' she said sharply.

'. . . All right.'

'OK. So. Here's the riddle. You're driving in the rain,' Grandma said, 'and you see three people waiting at a bus stop. They're getting soaked, but you only have space for one person in your car. As you pull up to them, you realise straight away that the three people are these. A sick elderly lady, who you think will die if she doesn't get out of the cold. Your favourite superhero, who is invincible to everything *except* for rain. And the person who knows you better than anyone.'

I thought. I had to admit, this interested me a little bit.

'So you're driving in the rain,' I said, 'and you see these other people who need to get out of it. There's the grandma . . .'

'Gran— whoa!' said Grandma crossly. 'I said "sick elderly lady", thank you very much!'

I began to laugh.

'What superhero gets hurt by *rain*?' said Stef with a giggle.

'Toilet Paper Man, innit,' Dimi said, and we all laughed, even Grandma. Then, suddenly, she leaned forwards and stopped the car.

'Oh no,' she said. 'Wait here.'

'What?' I said . . .

And then I saw it all.

I saw our flat. I saw an official-looking woman with a badge and a clipboard taping a notice to the front door, '*SECTION 21*' marked on it in red letters. I saw my mum and dad, both in their work clothes, looking tired and afraid, and *ashamed*. I saw Grandma hurrying over to join them, her voice rising in volume, sounding more Jamaican, which she gets when she's either very happy or very angry, and I saw that she definitely wasn't happy.

And I saw him. I saw Mr Stringer.

That's when I got out of the car.

'Padraig, Cynthia, I'm very sorry,' he was saying, smirking, not sounding sorry at all. 'I told the Council about the problems you've caused, and they decided that the best next step was eviction.'

'Padraig's *fixed* the roof, you horrible man,' Grandma shouted. 'He's *done* all the work on the ceiling, and since when did they damage the *roof*?! When did the Council even decide this?! When?!'

She rounded on the official-looking woman, but Mr Stringer stepped in between them.

'You don't need to harass her,' Mr Stringer warned, an ugly smile on his face. 'This flat's unsafe. I have to look after my *paying* tenants, don't I?'

That did it. Mum finally snapped.

'But we DO PAY!' she shouted. 'Why can't you just leave us alone! We have done NOTHING but bend over backwards, you STUPID MAN, and you are just HORRIBLE every time!'

She kept shouting, then Mr Stringer turned one way and saw Grandma, with that steely gaze of hers, turned the other way and saw my dad, who *never* loses his temper, except when somebody upsets my mum, or me, or . . . *or Celestine* . . .

Where was Celestine?

She was writing you a sorry note, if you must know.

'Dad,' I said.

Dad turned to me.

'Where's Celestine?' I said. 'Why hasn't she come out?'

'She's in your room,' Dad said, 'writing *you* a sorry note, before you get annoyed.'

It took a moment for this to go through my head. I heard my friends behind me, saying my name. I saw my parents, my grandma, all of them arguing with Mr Stringer, and suddenly their argument wasn't important right now. I walked forwards, then I ran, past everyone, through the front door, up the stairs, and barrelled into my room.

'I'm just writing a sorry note for Kyan,' Celestine said. She was kneeling on the floor, leaning on the Infinite Race box to write. 'I wasn't going to take anything.'

'You wouldn't write a sorry note for me,' I said. 'And no *way* would you leave here without taking something.'

I stepped forwards . . . and Celestine *shrank*, *bent backwards* . . . and *disappeared* into the box!

I walked towards the box, and crouched over it. It still looked old from the outside, still showed planes, trains and animals all riding along a track. But there was a little button-sized projector in the middle of it, a tiny video beaming out of it, growing until it was all around me. This was a new Infinite Race, with a new title.

THE INFINITE RACE ... X

New and Improved, with Holographic Distraction Field and 20% Quicker Hopping!!!

'Holographic distraction field,' I whispered, and looked closely at the projected video. *I* was in the video now, kneeling next to Celestine. Then I saw what was on the other side of the box and my heart skipped a beat.

The track was out.

Only it wasn't even a track right now. It was a dusty road. Tiny strings flew up, as though they were being kicked up. Hovering above the middle of it was a horse, *a toy horse*, and as I heard the faintest of screams, the others burst in through my bedroom door.

'We're just writing a sorry note,' I heard my voice echo around me. 'We're not misbehaving at all . . .'

I staggered to my feet and stepped out of the Holographic Field, and it must've been a shock, because Stef, Luke and Dimi all leaped back with a yell.

'Celestine's Hopped and it's all my fault,' I said.

20

'On a horse?!' said Luke. 'No. Way. You are *not* going alone.'

I looked from Luke, to Dimitar, to Stefania. They all shook their heads, determined. Outside, the argument with Mr Stringer was still going legendary.

'You *have* to stay here,' I said. 'Once my parents come up, they'll—'

'They'll just see us in that new distraction thingy!' said Luke. I sighed, and looked at the tiny projector. It now showed all of us, kneeling around the box, writing quietly.

'I mean, it's amazing, but how many sorry notes could we all be writing?'

'What did you tell me when Luke was missing?' Dimitar

said. 'Grown-ups won't believe what the track *could* be, anyway. And at least if we're in there with you, whatever Stringer wasteman comes for you, we can jog up and help.'

I didn't think horses jogged, but there wasn't time to argue. I had to pick a horse from Celestine's metal horse collection. There wasn't much to choose from:

- A short, squat horse, with a grumpy look.
- A unicorn, with a disdainful look.
- A purple pony, with a purple look.
- A light brown horse, with a livid look, and a long mohawk, or haircut, or whatever it's called.

So I tried to picture how *Celestine* would see them. The horsey show she loves came into my mind, *Rosalita's Riding School* – the one I *hate*, of course – and suddenly I twigged. The toy horse currently floating above the dusty track looked *really* like Rosalita's horse Fireheart. And the light brown angry-looking horse with the mohawk looked *just* like . . .

'Bonita Bee,' I said out loud. 'Anabella's horse. If anything can catch Fireheart, it's her.'

OK, so maybe I don't hate Celestine's horse cartoon as much as all that. You know what though? Everybody else nodded like they knew exactly what I was talking about, so *blatantly* they don't hate it either. The others chose their horses, and we got ready to ride.

'Now, remember what it was like,' I said. 'You need to *run*.'

'*Really* run,' said Luke fervently. 'You know, like *run*-run. *Run* run run.'

I nodded, and placed Bonita Bee on the track.

Only Bonita Bee didn't rev up, she *woke* up! She stumbled forwards with an angry snort and *grew* as I shrank – not smoothly, not like the cars and spaceship had, but jerkily, muscles bulging out, lurching me from side to side. She snorted again, grunted even more angrily, and by the time she was up to my shoulders, I could see that anger was meant for *me*. She shook her head left and right, trying to throw off my hand that was *stuck* gripping her floppy top-hair, slamming me into her gut, then the floor, then the other side of the floor, then . . .

'I don't like horses,' I said, with a horrible realisation.

There was a sucking sound . . .

I was wearing a long white cloak that wrapped around my

body, and wrapped *underneath* my horse, Bonita Bee. Oh, and I knew it wrapped underneath Bonita Bee because right now I was upside down, staring at Bonita Bee's bottom. The rocky ground raced beneath me, stones and spiky plants whipping my head, hot dust billowing painfully into my eyes and nose. With an angry grunt that sounded like she was trying to cough up a greenie, Bonita Bee – who didn't seem flipping *bonita* at all – kicked out her back legs, missed my face by a hair, and sent me tumbling to the . . .

'Nonono!' I shouted, and flailed out, desperate not to fall from Bonita and return home. Somehow one hand caught the white fabric of my cloak, and with one boot skidding through dirt and strings, I pulled myself back up on to the horse with a whimper.

'Isn't this great!' yelled Stefania, horse-sprinting past me. Her unicorn no longer had a horn sprouting from its face, but it hadn't lost its brilliant white paint job or its snooty expression. Beyond those smuggins, Dimi was bouncing along on his muscular steed with the same swagger he has on the football pitch.

'Me and Dimi go horse riding near my cousin Bunic's farm every summer in Romania!' Stefania continued happily. 'But Romania doesn't have three suns like this place, Kyan. THREE SUNS! JUST LOOK AT THE WEATHER SYSTEMS!'

She was pointing at a storm cloud nearby. Actually, 'storm cloud' doesn't do it justice. This was a never-ending storm the size of a city, black rolling clouds and blue lightning bolts that reached beyond the sky.

'Have you even *seen* a storm like that before?!' she shouted. 'This is AMAZING!'

'There's something wrong with you,' I said, but Stefania had already ridden ahead, leaning in close to her snootycorn and whispering.

Maybe that's how it works, I thought, then crawled up to Bonita's ears, and tried to whisper as sweetly as I could, dribble spilling from my mouth along with my rasping words.

'*Bonita Bee, my name is Kyan and I am your friend—*'

With a phlegmy grunt, Bonita STAMPED one horse-foot hard. I bounced up on her back, was airborne for a good second, and crunched back down, right on my privates.

'Ooooh,' I groaned in pain. 'Oooooooooh . . .'

'If you're "ooh"-ing, you're breathing!' yelled Luke cheerfully, as he rode up alongside me, sat with both legs to one side of his purple pony. 'Thank you, Dad, for three years of Pony Club!' But when he looked to me, his eyes widened in shock. 'Watch out, Kyan!'

'*You* watch out,' I said haughtily, forcing myself upright. 'You don't need to worry about me, I'll be – AAAARGH!'

Another horse was racing alongside us. On that horse was a boy about our age, his skin slightly darker than mine, as comfortable on his horse as I felt in an F1 racecar. He was wearing a white wrap too, up and around his head and billowing back in the wind.

Oh, and next to my right ear, close enough to clean it out if Bonita jerked up again, the boy held a sharp metal arrow on the string of a long, deadly-looking bow.

'HALT!' he shouted.

'Wait, please don't shock my horse I—'

'HALT!'

'You don't understand, she's evil, she—'

'HALT!'

'I CAN'T!' I wailed. 'I DON'T KNOW HOW!'

With a scowl, the boy reached out, placed three fingers on Bonita Bee's side, and she *stopped*, just like that. I slammed forwards, my face mashing into Bonita's manky mullet, and lay there.

'Celestine!' I groaned. 'You couldn't test-drive a scooter?!'

'Celestine?!' the boy said, his scowl softening. He lowered his bow. 'Are . . . are you Kyan? I am Yamnaya. I . . . I thought you were a Sparks Raider. Your sister is catching up with us now.'

Because I hadn't been humiliated enough, galloping towards us was my little sister, riding her horse Fireheart like a natural. With a delighted yell, that to a worried big brother might sound like a scream, she galloped faster than a racecar, and skidded to a halt, right next to me.

'Celestine,' I said, voice muffled by Bonita's mohawk. 'I've come to rescue you!'

Nobody looked convinced.

'No arguments,' I said to Celestine. 'Jump off that horse, and we'll all go home.'

'Er, *no*. What are you even doing here?' said Celestine.

I was *livid*. No explanations. No thanks. No apologies for using my Infinite Racetrack – and not even with cars, but with *these* devil creatures.

'Do you know how scared I was?' I said. 'You'd disappeared! I thought I heard you screaming from inside the game! You could've been anywhere!'

'Oh really?' Celestine said, her annoyance turning

to anger. 'And what about when *I* was scared? What about when *you'd* disappeared? You called me a snitch! You said everyone would've been happier without me!'

I . . . didn't have an answer for that. Yamnaya and my friends all horse-sidled away awkwardly. Celestine had tried following me, had tried to get involved, and I'd just ignored her. I was supposed to be her brother, someone she could be honest with in a way she couldn't always be honest to Mum and Dad, someone she could rely on in a way she couldn't always rely on her friends, someone she . . .

'Someone she knows better than anyone,' I murmured. 'Huh.' I sat up a little bit straighter, and to my enormous relief, Bonita Bee didn't throw me to the floor and stamp on my head.

'You're . . . right,' I said. 'I've been horrible. I thought I could save our home, and then . . . I messed it up, and wanted to blame you because it was easier. I . . . I'm sorry.'

That word wasn't getting easier to say. But Celestine's anger subsided.

'But, *honest*,' I continued, 'we need to go back now. Mr Stringer's literally in the middle of kicking us out. We're losing our home.'

'I know we're losing our home,' Celestine said. 'You said the Infinite Race was the only way to save us. I've been trying to get it to work all afternoon. And now, *Kyan*, I don't know how, but *I fixed it.*'

'Well, technically, Celestine . . .' I began. Bonita Bee looked sharply up at me. *Can she understand English?!* I thought uneasily. 'Technically . . . yeah! You did fix it! But *this isn't the world we need.* We have to find a race, something with a big prize. Look around. They've got no money here.'

'But then shouldn't we help them save their home even more?'

I stared at my sister. She stared stubbornly back. Yamnaya began to horse-amble back over.

'You didn't tell him we're from another dimension, did you?' I murmured.

'Give me some credit!'

'Oh, phew.'

'I told him we're from a town called Bedroom.'

'. . . Good thinking,' I said. Sometimes it's just nice to be nice. I saw the determination on Celestine's face, the worry on Yamnaya's, and as he reached us, I sighed. Spider Ace *had* told us to leave the worlds better than we found them.

'OK,' I said. 'What's the problem in this dimension?'

266

* * *

'My village is up ahead,' Yamnaya said. 'At least, it *will* be, so long as the Sparks Raiders don't destroy it.'

'How would you tell if they did?' I murmured to Luke.

We were riding through harsh, endless desert; jagged land surrounded by steep cliffs and a never-ending sky. I couldn't see houses, or even huts. The towering storm ahead of us didn't exactly help the view either. It was epic in size, thundering chundering clouds that looked more violent the closer we got. Crazily, an old woman was crawling along the ground in front of the cloud, searching for something. *Oh, they must have nothing here*, I thought pityingly. I peered down to see what she might be picking up, and saw a moving brown carpet of rust-coloured bugs. *She has to eat bugs!* I thought, feeling even more sorry for her. *Oh, these poor, poor people.*

I felt pretty sorry for myself too. Stefania had been right about the suns. Not one, not two, but *three* were beating down on us, and I shifted uncomfortably in my saddle, trying miserably to make my shawl float around me in the same cooling way it seemed to do for Yamnaya, Celestine and soon even the others. But the sweat only grew worse, stinging my eyes and dripping down on to

Bonita Bee, making her snort with every single drip like it was *my* fault. As we trudged along, the huge storm tower grew closer, more threatening, and I began to wonder just where Yamnaya's village could be.

'Nearly there,' he said, as though reading my thoughts. 'It's probably not as nice as Bedroom though.' The shy way he said it made me think of the first time I'd realised how big Luke's house was. He was nervous. He didn't want me to laugh at his home.

'I doubt it,' I said, as kindly as I could. 'We haven't got nearly as many, um, pebbles in Bedroom. Hey, just to warn you, there's a great big storm cloud over there.'

Yamnaya smiled politely but strangely, like what I'd said didn't make sense. The dark, foreboding cloud came closer. Stef, Dimi and Luke were up ahead with Celestine, and though I couldn't hear what she was saying, she pointed at the storm calmly, as though there was no problem with it at all.

'Er, guys?' I said, but a loud CRACK of rolling thunder drowned me out. I felt the air drop, suddenly cooler. Starting to panic, I tried pushing Bonita's head to the side in the hope that she would turn away from the cloud. Fat chance. She snapped her teeth at my fingers, making me flinch back with a mini-shriek that made Yamnaya glance back strangely again.

My sister and my friends reached the cloud and . . .
entered it!

'Celestine!'

*They're hypnotised. Everyone's hypnotised by the storm,
and they've just walked into their doom and now I'm going
there too because of a horse that hates me and* . . .

I hit the storm cloud with a wet SLAP!

'ARGH!' I shrieked. 'ARRGH! ARGHHHHHHH! . . .
Argh?'

For a moment I saw nothing but cloud, heard nothing
but the roar of thunder, wind and rain. Then the storm
subsided. The mist brightened, softened into white candy-
floss, unbelievably refreshing after the searing heat of
three suns. I heard the gentle sound of water, then as the
mist cleared I looked around and . . .

'Yamnaya,' I said. 'You live in paradise!'

21

We were on top of a hill, looking down into a basin-shaped valley. Tropical-looking trees grew all around us, with thick trunks and wide leaves that hummed gently as we passed. Beneath our horsefeet, babbling brooks rushed out from the white cloud wall, blue sparks zipping along them as they did. In the distance, clusters of wooden huts poked out from between the trees, their thick wooden beams tied together with a gently glowing rope-like plant.

'My village,' Yamnaya said. 'Right in the Mighty Eye.'

'It's amazing,' I said, 'I mean it – amazing!'

With a proud smile, Yamnaya led us on, following the babbling brooks as they wound their way downhill. Soon

they merged together into larger streams, until they all came together to form a fat, crawling river. The air actually tasted sweet, and even that miserable nag Bonita gave a lip-smacking satisfied grumble, the kind of noise Dimi makes with pudding till we tell him he's freaking out the other kids at the table. I felt a cold drop of water on the back of my hand, and looked up. The cloud wall we had just travelled through curved gently around us as it reached up to the sky, as if we were looking up out of a giant woolly sock, one sun peering over the edge like a happy big toe.

'Weather systems, dude,' Stef said. 'Weather systems. The three suns heat up water until it evaporates into vapour. When the vapour lifts, it gets colder, and the tiny water droplets rub together, making static electricity. On our planet, the lifting vapour would cause really heavy winds, and the static electricity would want to jump to the ground as lightning, and the water droplets would fall as—'

'Rain!' said Luke, as another single droplet of water fell on his hand. We looked up again, but no more fell.

'On this planet though,' Stefania continued, 'the other suns must heat the water vapour back up just at the right time. The storm stays in one place and stretches out, and because the eye is so big and is here for so long, it makes a mini ecosystem in the desert, a tropical paradise where people can live. They've even figured out a way to stop the sparks in the water from shocking us, probably with these cloaks. They might even use the electricity!'

'Electricity?' I said, dropping my voice to a murmur. 'Come off it, Stef, everyone rides horses. This woman was collecting bugs to ... Mmm, that smells amazing! Hey Yamnaya, what's that cooking—?'

I stopped short as we reached a hut, nestled by the river. Standing in front of it, the elderly woman I'd seen gathering bugs outside the storm reached into her bag and tossed a handful of bugs into a big pan. The pan sizzled, sparks fizzed and danced out of it, and the smell – which was more delicious than bugs should ever smell – wafted out even stronger than before. Only ... this pot wasn't resting on a fire, I realised. It was sitting on a pile of these tree leaves, and they were glowing.

But yo, that wasn't even what got me shook. What was proper amazing, was the canvas that hung on a line above the pan. It looked like it had been woven from the same plant that tied the huts together, and as the bugs crackled and fizzed in the pot, the sparks that danced up from them seemed to soak up into the fabric ... and a video of somebody else cooking appeared on it.

273

'It's a recipe video,' I squeaked with amazement. 'Like . . . like a TV! Yamnaya, you have TV! Wait, does that mean you have . . . ?'

Not listening, Yamnaya had climbed down from his horse, and was jogging up to the old woman, taking out his own ball of leaf-fabric from his pocket as he did.

'Salem, Botai!' he called to the old woman.

'Salem, Yamnaya,' she replied with a grin. 'You want some bug juice to charge that Sparks Wrap?'

'Ah, Botai,' Yamnaya said, grinning himself. 'How can I get anything past you?'

Botai laughed.

'You can try charging that thing,' she said finally, 'but you know it won't last. You need a new wrap!'

Yamnaya held the Sparks Wrap over the pot, letting the sparks soak up into it. Soon it flattened out like a snap band, and a loading screen appeared!

'Thanks, Botai!' Yamnaya said. At a smiling nod from her, he grabbed a bug out from the pot and jogged back to join us.

'Tablets,' I said faintly. 'You've got tablets. What a wonderful world this is.'

'You mean the Sparks Wrap? Hmph, when it holds its charge,' Yamnaya grumbled.

He handed it to me, and eagerly I swiped at the canvas. Just like my tablet, a series of menus swooshed past . . . until blue sparks fizzed from the 'screen', and the Sparks Wrap fell limp in my hands, just a piece of fabric again.

'Aw, nuts,' Yamnaya sighed. 'See? All the jobs I have to do just for an hour on this stupid thing and still it never works right.'

'I feel your pain,' I said meaningfully, as he climbed nimbly back on to his horse. We carried on past Botai's hut to where a long, wide wooden bridge crossed the river. Yamnaya broke the cooked bug into pieces and offered some around, and while Celestine, Luke and Dimi all shook their heads, green-gilled, me and Stef both took a piece. It tasted amazing, like cinnamon crisps, and my tongue danced with the electricity it left behind.

'I mean, I get what my dads are always saying,' Yamnaya said through chews, as our horses stepped slowly on to the bridge. 'If we do the easy thing and take the water and the food from inside the storm, it'll lose energy and collapse. Just . . . it always seems to end up being me who has to collect the sparks first, "because YOU'RE the oldest".'

'Kyan gets that too,' Celestine said. I looked at her, so shocked that she grinned.

'Why would taking the electricity out of your storm destroy it?' Dimi asked.

'Any system needs energy to work,' said Stef. 'A storm's the same – if you take too much energy out before the sun puts it in, it will collapse.'

'Pops said that's what happened to the Sparks Raiders' home storm,' Yamnaya said. 'They used up all of their energy, and rather than let their storm recharge, they stole everyone else's.'

'Stole them?' I asked. 'How?'

'It's scary – we don't know,' Yamnaya admitted. 'We had thought they were cutting the leaves from our trees or cooking the Sparks Bugs, like we do. But the trees aren't even touched when they attack, and they're stealing big figure sparks, too many to get from bugs. Instead, they race through the town on these machines I've never even seen before, smashing our huts until we chase them. Then, while we're chasing them, their leader leeches tonnes of sparks from the storm.'

'Who's their leader?' Dimi asked.

'All I know is that the Sparks Raiders call him "Killer K",' Yamnaya said. 'We don't even know how they're getting in here – we've been patrolling the outside of the storm for weeks, but if they take any more sparks the Mighty Eye will collapse.'

'What about the river?' Luke asked. 'Could they be travelling up that to get in?'

'Up the river?' Yamnaya repeated, and gave Luke the same odd look he'd given me when I tried to warn him about riding into the storm. 'All our rivers end at the Big Lake, and the Big Lake ends at the Currents. Don't yours?'

He pointed out over the side of the bridge, and I saw what he meant. The river we were crossing wasn't just a river any more. It, along with hundreds of other rivers and streams, was flowing into a great lake in the very centre of the storm's eye. The air was so clear that I could see around the edge of the lake for miles, loads of little bays with wooden jetties and rowboats gently bobbing beside them. Directly ahead of us, beyond the mouth of the river, a series of rocks glistened out across the water like a pier . . . but then they disappeared into a thick, white mist that hung over the very middle of the lake.

'In there?' Stef said. 'In that mist you mean is—'

'The Currents,' Yamnaya said, and there was fear in his voice. 'Where the rain falls up, and everything else falls down . . . and down. Last year I rode the Stepping Stones to explore the mist with my friends. By the time I caught sight of the Updraft, I thought I wasn't ever going to make it back. Pops and Dops raced out themselves to drag us back in, and grounded me for about a month. People have died searching the Currents. Any boat going there would crash down on the rocks below.'

'The rain falls up?' Luke exclaimed. 'Amazing! I didn't even think you had rain here, except for that bit of spitting when we first arrived.'

'Spitting rain?' Yamnaya said, suddenly very serious. 'Where? When?'

'. . . Just when we got here,' I said. 'I—'

Before he could answer, a series of harsh, buzzing roars ripped through the air around us. *Buzzzzzz! BUUUzzzzzz! BUZZZZZZZZZ!*

'That's them,' Yamnaya said fearfully. 'That's the Sparks Raiders.'

The sounds grew louder, sharper. They were coming behind us, I realised, and as I looked back I saw them race past the bridge; four helmeted Sparks Raiders on futuristic-looking motorbikes. There was a crash, and a shout of anguish.

'Get AWAY!' the voice shouted. 'Lousy villains, get AWAY!'

'Botai,' Yamnaya exclaimed. 'We've got to save Botai!'

22

*B*UZZZZZZZZZ! BUZZZ-BUUUZZZZZZZZZZZZ!
   'YAH!' Yamnaya cried, and chased back across
the bridge after the Sparks Raiders. Celestine didn't hesitate to follow.

'YAH!' she shouted. 'Go Fireheart, YAH!' Fireheart
didn't hesitate, rearing around on his hind legs and racing
back along the bridge towards Botai's hut. With determined hollers my friends all followed.

'YAH!' I shouted to Bonita, squeezing my legs and
pointing a finger after them. 'YAH!'

But try as I might, that wretched horse wouldn't move.
She cocked her head, as though listening out for something,
took three sideways steps towards the water, and waited.

'What?!' I said. 'What are you doing now?! Backwards! Reverse—'

With a sudden speed that sent me toppling back, Bonita bolted forwards the wrong way across the bridge!

'NO!' I cried desperately. 'HEEL! AMSCRAY! UNDERLAY!'

It was no good. Reaching the wrong side of the bridge, that blummin' horse veered a sharp right. We flew between huts, skipped past cookpots and through washing lines. We jumped fences, and tore beneath trees hanging so low that I had to pin myself to Bonita's horse-mullet to avoid being ripped off her. And finally we skidded a sharp right again, and burst out on to a rocky shore, where there was nothing but a hut and—

'LAKE LAKE RIVER RIVER!' I shrieked, as we flew towards the water. Bonita skidded to a halt, so quickly that the white cloak wrapped around my head and I face-planted her mohawk again.

'Youuuu . . .' I seethed, clawing my white cloak from my face as I gulped for air. 'Good young horses don't act like that with their—'

Bonita grunted, and I knew what she'd said.

'You shushed me! You shushed me!'

That's when I heard a hushed voice coming from the other side of that hut. It was cruel, sneering and cold.

And it was almost familiar.

'If I wanted you to think, Sims,' sneered Killer K, aka Chief Stringer, aka Kenneth Tha Goat, aka Mr Stringer, 'I would jimjammerin' pay you better. These sparks'll give us power for weeks.'

'That's him,' I whispered. 'Stringer is Killer K!' Bonita Bee took a half-step forwards, allowing me to lean out and peer around the wooden walls.

Beyond the hut, sitting calmly on the quick waters that flowed from the river mouth into the Big Lake, was a craft so out of this world that it took me a moment to twig that it was a boat. It was made from gleaming metal, so thin that it looked like tinfoil twisted into the shape of a paper bird, the word *Euphoria* stamped across the hull. The deck was made of black glass, and instead of a throttle or a wheel, there was just a single black orb. And on the riverbank beside this crazy yacht, two familiar figures were arguing.

'And what happens when we use all that power, Killer?' Sims, aka Navigator Sima, aka Officer Sima, aka Announcer Sima retorted. 'This storm is ready to blow. Are we going to drain every dashblam' squall this side of the Peninsula?'

'You'll do everything I say if you want to get muttonpickin'' 'paid,' Killer K snapped. 'Now CHARGE THAT LAST BATTERY.' He moved, and I saw what he was talking about: four metal cylinders that reached up to his hip, literally the same shape as big AA batteries, even with big #pl signs on the bumpy end. Like his yacht the *Euphoria*, the batteries seemed light, but they crackled when Killer K lifted one in each hand, and as he carried them up the boarding ramp his hair stood on end. They were full of energy stolen from Yamnaya's storm.

'You ain't paid none of us yit,' Sima muttered, once he was out of earshot. But like in the first universe I visited,

she hadn't decided whether or not to do the right thing. After scowling at him a moment more, she lifted up the other two batteries and dangled them in the lake. The water around them glowed a bright, lightning blue, and for one moment, the air seemed to crackle with static.

If they took any more energy from the storm, it would collapse, Yamnaya had said. Suddenly it started to happen. There was a crack of thunder, so loud it shivered my teeth. The clouds above us began to swirl, faster and faster, closing in on the eye of the storm. Fat, cold drops of rain began to fall, single splashes at first, then a heavy shower. A howl of wind picked up, and when lightning flashed across the horizon, even Killer K seemed to realise what he'd done.

'Time to roll out,' he hollered to Sims.

'What about the others?' she protested.

'They can catch us at the Thermal.'

With that Killer K turned and traced his hand across the control orb. There was a quiet whoosh, eerie lights glowed beneath the tinfoil hull, and even as Sims leaped on board with the other two batteries in her hands, even as the *Buzz-Buuzzzzzz!* echoed across the other side of the bridge, followed by the clatterclatter of hoofs chasing them, Killer K's yacht the *Euphoria* zoomed away from the shore and out towards the lake.

'We've got to warn the others!' I exclaimed. Suddenly, an idea occurred to me. 'The Metamorphic Headphones! They might have turned into a walkie-talkie.' I reached down my shirt and pulled out . . .

A whistle. A wooden whistle. Muttering about this universe – and Kyan Green's lousy stuff in every universe – I put it to my lips and blew.

WOOOOOOOO! The whistle vibrated through my white cloak, spreading it wide like phoenix wings. I pulled it out from my mouth in shock, and a blue, blinding beam of light shone out of it, up into the darkening sky. For a split second I heard the distant noise of the Sparks Raiders' attack quieten. Then, with the *buzzzz* of motorbikes turning around, headlights burst out along the wooden bridge, swiftly chased by a group of horses with Celestine and Fireheart at the lead.

'Go it, the Tines!' I cheered. But as I pointed the blue light of my whistletorch out across the water I saw they would be too late to catch Killer K. His tinfoil yacht *Euphoria* had turned away from the river mouth already, and was aimed directly for the darkening mist in the centre of the Big Lake. They were headed for the

Currents, and there was only one horse who could catch them.

'Bonita,' I urged, leaning forwards to speak into her ear. 'You don't like me, and I don't like you. But if we don't catch that boat this whole storm will collapse. Now chase that – AAAAAARGH!'

Bonita didn't even wait for my command. She sped forwards, sending me floundering back like an inflatable car wash man. Rain and swirling winds whipped across my face as we galloped along the rocky shore. The storm was collapsing, the Mighty Eye was shrinking, and the skies turned black. Even with my mega whistletorch I could barely make out the *Euphoria* ... until lightning illuminated the lake to show that we were neck and neck! But we were on land and they were on the water, headed straight for the lake's centre. There was only one way we could catch them there.

'Bonita!' I yelled. 'The Stepping Stones!'

She was way ahead of me. We banked right again, Bonita leaping from the pebble beach to the glistening rocks that led out across the lake, galloping furiously for the Currents. Leaning forwards, bouncing in time with the rhythm of her run, I felt a different kind of speed, as exhilarating as any ship or car I had driven so far. We were halfway to the thick fog ahead and I was certain we'd make it!

That's when the angry buzzing of Sparks Raiders ripped out behind me.

A bolt of green laser fire blasted past us through the mist and spray and I ducked down, urging Bonita to go faster, faster, faster. Still another bolt flew past us, barely missing my left ear, and as the pale glow of Killer K's *Euphoria* disappeared into the fog of the Currents, the roar of Sparks Raider motorbikes threatened to burst my eardrums, and the leader burst out on to the rocks alongside me, aiming his blaster for Bonita!

'No!' I cried. But before he could fire, an arrow whistled through the air and exploded the Raider's back tyre, sending the bike flipping forwards!

'Quickly, Kyan, ride, ride!' I heard Yamnaya yell after me.

Another bike buzzed forwards after us, but the three-beat of galloping hoofs raced up alongside them, forcing them off the rocky pier and into the water.

'Go Kyan! Go Kyan! Go Kyan!' Celestine shouted, as Fireheart reared up in triumph at the other terrified Sparks Raiders.

'Yes, Tines, you saved my neck!' I whooped. And then

we plunged into the mist of the Currents, and my grin faded.

Thick and angry, the dark fog hit my sight like a slap, swallowing the light from my whistletorch after just a few metres. The sound of waterfalls surrounded us, a thousand cymbals that twisted my head, turning left into right and up into down. When the rocky path began to break up into stepping stones, Bonita slowed to a canter . . . then to a walk. Only when I caught the occasional glimpse of fast-flowing water below, or of that pale-blue glow of Killer K's *Euphoria* ahead, did I even know we weren't just going around in circles. Thunder clattered through me, and wind ripped the rain like scratches across my face. Above me, lightning crackled so close the heat threatened to scorch my scalp. Below me, sparks tore violently through the water, spraying out mini-shocks like scattering hot needles that burned my skin and made the alarmed Bonita whimper with pain.

'Don't give up,' I whispered. 'It'll be OK.' But I was lying. Down here, in the Currents, where it seemed like the whole universe was collapsing around me, things seemed far from OK. As the Stepping Stones grew sharper, and further apart, Bonita was forced to leap, skid and stop on each one, before even attempting to make the next jump.

Minutes went past without even seeing the glow of the *Euphoria*, and all my hope gave way to despair. Yamnaya had been right. Nobody would survive long down here. Killer K had lured us in, just to see us smash on the rocks.

And then a huge lightning bolt hissed through the water beside us. It traced between the Stepping Stones ahead, raced alongside a long, thin runway of rock after them, lit up the crackling static air – and revealed the *Euphoria*, closer than ever.

'OVER THERE!' I shouted, and Bonita burst into a canter. She skipped once, twice across the next two stones, before leaping for the runway of rock. Almost as soon as we landed, I noticed that things had changed suddenly. The air here was hot, and the rain was upside down, fat drops of water flying upwards towards the sky. My hair and white cloak lifted, and a wet gale whipped up my nostrils, that warm air getting hotter and hotter, and spiralling around me as it did. Bonita noticed the grotty sensation too, but though she snickered and snorted angrily, still she picked up into a run. The *Euphoria* was bobbing and bouncing gently between the rocks ahead of us like a stick in a stream. At that speed we could catch it, I thought, and my hopes lifted like the rain.

Then I saw the sunlight beaming down intensely into the chasm ahead of us, and they died again.

There must've been a thousand waterfalls at least, awesome and deadly; all plunging water deep into the ground right at the heart of the Mighty Eye, just before the intense heat of three suns lifted it back up. This was what Killer K had called the Thermal, and Yamnaya had called the Updraft; a current of burning hot air, heated by those three suns high above us hitting one point – an invisible elevator so powerful it made upside-down rain. We raced closer to the edge of the rock just as Killer K's *Euphoria* yacht plunged over the edge of the waterfall, disappeared from view . . . and then reappeared.

Suddenly I saw how clever that boat really was. Its hull was so light, that rather than plunge down into the chasm below, it sank slowly, light enough to be supported by the Updraft. It got cleverer still. As Killer K traced his hand over the control orb, those tinfoil wings began to unfold, stretching out wider and wider. As the glider yacht caught more of the rising air it lifted back up, slowly circling the Thermal until it was nearly level with us again.

'No,' I whispered. Bonita wasn't quitting, we raced ever faster, the thunder of her hoofs as loud in my mind as the thunder above. But she was much too slow – how could she ever leap that far, far enough to catch a flying ship?

It's not a flying ship, a sarky-smart voice echoed through my head (you know it was Stef's). *It's a glider.* And with the edge of the rock racing towards us, as lightning again lit up the air, I had an idea that was crazy.

'RIGHT, BONITA!' I yelled. 'YOU DON'T LIKE ME AND I DON'T LIKE YOU. BUT IF YOU MAKE THAT JUMP, I'LL HELP YOU FLY!'

Slowly, unsteadily, I began to rise, until I was crouched on my feet, teeth gritted, sweat dripping upwards from my forehead.

'FOUR!' I shouted as the precipice raced towards us. 'THREE! TWO . . .'

I didn't have time for 'one'. Bonita leaped from the rock, and I leaped up from her, spreading my arms and holding my cloak out as wide as I could. We flew through the rising air, Bonita Bee and her human hang-glider, never soaring, but almost sailing, above a thousand plunging waterfalls, through the scorching heat of the Mighty Eye's core, all the way across to the *Euphoria*. I roared, all of the rage I felt at every Stringer across existence bellowing out from the back of my throat, and as Sima and Killer K whirled around to see a horse flying through the air towards them, Killer K let out a scream—

'IT CAN'T BE!'

Then Bonita hit the deck. Her heavy hoofs cracked the black glass, and the glider-boat jerked across the Thermal, whipping around into an awkward, tipping spin. I was yanked back down on to Bonita with a thump that knocked the breath out of me, and together we skidded across the deck. With a desperate roar of his own, Killer K swiped at his control orb, opening up the *Euphoria*'s wings even more.

It was the worst thing he could've done. We whirli-gigged around the Thermal like a kite on fire. Storm clouds and destruction spun past us, Bonita slammed hard into the boat's barrier, and all we could do was crouch down low and hold tight. But Killer K had other ideas. Grabbing a laser blaster from his hip, he staggered across the deck towards us.

'YOU!' he snarled. 'YOU DID THI—'

It was all he got out. After one last spin, the *Euphoria* was flung out like a frisbee, out of the misty Currents, low above Big Lake. Killer K vanished, swept away by the wind and I screamed.

'BONITA, SAVE YOURSEL—' I roared, but was cut short as the ship *FLOOMed* down, a wave crashing up and sweeping us off the deck and into the water!

After the Thermal's heat, the Big Lake was an ice bath. I plunged down deep, swallowing bucketfuls, flailing and floundering in my white cloak, froth and bubbles and sparks and the universe crashing down above me. Everything was chaos, pitch-black and frightening. There was no hope of swimming back up. It was just too deep. It was just too cold. And I was just too tired.

Then I felt my white cloak pull . . . and pull again.

Slow, exhausted, I began to pull back. One hand after another, I hoisted myself forwards and up, up through the cold waters of Big Lake, my lungs swelling inside my chest. At last, when they were about to burst, I looped one exhausted arm over Bonita's shoulders, and without hesitating she hefted me up, out of the water, gulping down oxygen with every shuddering breath.

She'd done it. That miserable horse had saved me.

'Nyer!' I gasped, trying to thank her but completely out of breath. 'Thlem. Mmneyer!' Giving up at last, I lay forwards on Bonita's back, and shivered in the rain.

Only . . . that rain was dying. As Bonita climbed back ashore, I looked up and saw why.

The *Euphoria* was sinking beneath the water, and the charged batteries were drifting away. The energy was spilling back out of them, a spreading pool of blue light that fizzed and danced across the water before disappearing. As the last battery leaked the last of its energy, disappearing beneath the water, the rain stopped all together. Me and Bonita stood there, both of us breathing hard and shivering, taking in the sweet, fresh air as the whistling wind fell away.

'We did it,' I said, amazed. 'We put all the energy back into the storm.'

'Not all of it,' a voice said behind me.

It was Killer K. His head was bleeding, and he was limping badly. But in his hands was a laser blaster, like the ones the Sparks Raiders had been firing. It was pointed directly at us.

'First thing I do when we sneak into this storm?' he snarled. 'I use the sparks to charge up the jibliberrin' nit-twitcherin' BLASTERS.'

And with that, he pulled the trigger.

Nothing happened. He pulled it again. Still nothing happened.

'And I drained the power back out of it,' Sims said behind him.

'You . . . IDIOT!' Killer K said. 'WE NEED THIS! WE NEED ALL THIS POWER!'

'No we don't,' Sims said calmly. 'We want it.'

BAROO-BAROOOOOOON! The sound echoed around us, a deep horn that seemed to shine a beam of blue light directly down at us, like a reverse of my wooden whistle. There was a pause for a moment, and then a deep rumbling sound echoed across the lake towards us.

'Not another storm!' I said.

It wasn't. Suddenly riders burst out towards us from every side; fifty, then a hundred, then at least two hundred riders. They swarmed in, covered every possible escape route, and as he turned to see the rest of his Sparks Raiders trussed up alongside some of the horses, Killer K fell to his knees, and closed his eyes.

'Awwwwww, the Happy Corporation ain't gonna like this one bit,' he groaned.

'Who?' I said, suddenly interested. But before he could respond, I heard a yell of delight from a familiar friend.

'You did it!' Yamnaya said, as he reached us. 'You saved the day!'

'Ah, it was nothing . . .' I began . . . but he was talking to Bonita! As I sat there, feeling nuff embarrassed, Yamnaya murmured to Bonita, stroking her mullet and even nuzzling her. She didn't even bite his nose off! But before I even dared protest, my sister and my friends surrounded me.

'Kyan!'

'What happened?!'

'You should've seen me I took out this one guy like POW and then this other guy like—'

'KYAAAAAN!' a familiar voice bellowed down the hill towards us, and we all froze. 'CELESTIIIIINE!' I looked up the bank, and saw her, riding her horse down the hill.

'Is that Grandma?!' Celestine said, fear crossing her face.

'Mmmmm, almost,' I said. 'I'll explain later.'

'I said to go to the next storm and ask for help fighting the Raiders,' Almost-Grandma yelled from up the hill. 'Not for you to form a spark-shankerin' posse!'

'The same goes for you two!' another familiar voice said, this universe's version of Mrs Anev. 'Trying to take on Killer K alone!'

'And you,' a stern voice said nearby. I turned again and saw Other Luke's dad crossing the wooden bridge.

'I think this is the bit we're allowed to miss,' Stefania whispered to us. I nodded.

'Yamnaya,' I began, 'we're gonna ... well, we're not going, but—'

'Wait.' He cut me off. 'First, let me give you all something before we're all grounded for a very long time.'

He handed me a pouch. My friends trotted close alongside me, huddling in to look as I opened the pouch . . . and gasped. There, glittering inside, was an assortment of precious stones and gold.

'I know, I know,' Yamnaya said apologetically. 'What would anybody want with a bunch of rocks just from the ground, eh? But . . . even though they don't compare to an adventure or a friend or a game on a Sparks Wrap, I've always thought they looked pretty cool.'

'. . . They're amazing,' Celestine breathed. 'Kyan, these could save our . . .'

I nodded, unable to speak. I looked up at Yamnaya, and held out my fist. I don't think they did that in this universe, since he smiled, awkwardly, before bumping it. Then, making him look even more confused, I tipped roughly half of the gemstones and gold out of the pouch, and placed them into his hand.

'This sounds weird, but can you give us the rest of these in a minute?' I said.

'Thank you, Yamnaya,' Celestine said, her voice tight like she was going to cry. 'And thank you too, Fireheart.'

'Oh,' Stefania said, and she looked at Celestine, then Fireheart, then her own snooty white horse with dismay. 'Oh . . . of course.' After a moment she abruptly leaned down close to whisper something herself. Soon my friends were all leaning forwards, whispering their own horse-goodbyes.

'Wow,' Yamnaya said. 'You guys really like your horses!'

Looking down at Bonita, I leaned in as well.

'Thank you, Bonita Bee,' I whispered. And as I lifted one leg over her back, my foot catching in the stirrup again; as I slipped and flailed like a soft toy, before pulling myself free with a desperate whimper and dropping; and as the ground became strings and swallowed me up –

Bonita Bee gave me a vindictive look, and let out a massive trump. And I *knew* – just *knew* – one thing.

I do not like horses.

We plunged through strings. Other universes flew by. I saw a sports car, a familiar face sitting in it. Spider Ace almost smiled which, judging from what she'd been like when we met her, was probably a big deal. The strings bunched together. The world formed, making shapes I knew; a light, a bed, a . . .

CRASH!

'Ohhh,' I groaned. 'These re-entries are getting worse.'

I looked around me. Dimitar was on his back, staring at the ceiling; Stefania was struggling to her feet with a groan. Luke was on his face, lifting his head . . . then dropping again with a grunt. And Celestine . . . I couldn't see her.

'Celestine? Celestine?' I got to my feet, suddenly scared. 'Celestine!'

'Here,' came her voice. She was sitting, perfectly comfortable, on the top of my high sleeper bed. I breathed a sigh of relief . . . then I saw she wasn't smiling.

'What's up?' I said. She shook her head.

'Fireheart's changed.'

'Changed?' I said. 'What do you mean?'

'I had it in my hands,' she said, 'I promise I did. It just . . . melts away. And Fireheart's changed.'

I knew what I'd see before I saw it. I knew . . . and still it hurt so much. Celestine handed me her toy Fireheart. On one side was a tiny metal pouch, painted brown with tiny painted treasure inside.

'We can't do it,' I said, and my voice sounded hollow. 'We can't get money from the Infinite Race.'

23

'No, Ken,' my dad was saying, and I could hear his gritted teeth through the living room door. 'I carried out those repairs. You've got to give us our deposit back.'

It was one hour later. My friends had all gone home, and I was stood with Celestine in the hallway, listening to our home being taken away.

'Now, Padraig,' Mr Stringer replied, a smirk in his voice. 'There are simply too many discrepancies! How can I give you this money back?'

'We *need* that money,' Mum said.

'That's the problem,' Mr Stringer said. 'I *don't* need it. I can wait long enough for the hurt your insults caused

301

me to heal, *Cynthia*. Isn't that right, Housing Officer Dabas?'

'Yes,' another voice said, 'but . . . Mr Stringer, I really need to go.'

There was the sound of footsteps approaching the door, and we ducked back into my room. The living room door opened, and footsteps hurried past, downstairs and out through our front door. Or, at least, what *used* to be our front door.

'I'm just going to be alone for a while,' Celestine said through tears. She left, and I sat on my bedroom floor alone, head down, unspeakably sad. My friends, my road, my park. I didn't know when, if ever, I would see them again.

'How's it going, little man?' said a voice from the door. It was Grandma. She hadn't called me that for ages.

'Fine, I guess,' I said, in a voice that didn't sound fine at all.

She stood and watched me, till I couldn't ignore her any more.

'I figured out your riddle,' I said. 'You know . . . You are driving in the rain, and you see three people waiting at a bus stop. They're getting soaked, but you only have space for one person in your car. There's the frail old grandma—'

'*Lady—*'

'There's that superhero, Toilet Paper Man. And there's the person who knows me better than anyone.'

'Well?' Grandma said. 'What was your answer? How do you get home?'

'What I'd do,' I said, 'is . . . I would let the elderly, er, woman get in the passenger seat, and then I'd give Papier Mâché man the keys to the car. *Then*, I would make my own way home with the people who know me best. Because it's the journey that matters.'

'You're a bright boy,' Grandma said. She sounded like she meant it.

'You told me that riddle to make me realise how important my sister is,' I said. 'Didn't you? And I get it. I . . . I really get it. But Celestine isn't the only one who knows me best. And if we move away from my friends, I'll . . . I'll always be on a different road to them. And what about Celestine's friends? And what about Mum and Dad? They're always so tired – how do I stop that? And what about you, Grandma? We can't move away from you—'

'Ky,' said Grandma, her voice Jamaican again. I looked up. She was smiling, her eyes shiny and bright. 'Sometimes . . . just be a child, nuh?' She gave me a hug, just like that.

After I wiped my eyes, she added, 'Besides, if it *is* about the journey . . . you're already richer than that stupid man Mr Stringer and his friend from the Council. Or . . . Kyan, what's the matter?'

Something had clicked.

'The woman from the Council,' I said slowly. 'What was her name?'

'Her name?!' Grandma said, and shrugged. 'I didn't catch it . . .'

But I was already running out of the room by then.

I looked up and down the street, but I couldn't see her at first. Then I felt a pair of eyes on me, turned, and caught her staring before she turned and walked quickly away.

'Mm-mm,' I said, shaking my head. 'Nope.' I ran after her, got till I was close, and shouted out.

'Your name's Sima, isn't it!'

'Kyan, what are you doing?!' Grandma shouted, hurrying towards us. But the woman had stopped, and turned to face me. It was her. It was Sima.

'You work for Mr Stringer, don't you?' I said to Sima. 'You're not really from the Council at all.'

'That's absurd,' Sima began, but then she saw the determination in my face, and stopped.

'I know . . .' I paused. Somehow it didn't seem like the

right moment to tell her about our meetings in other dimensions. 'I *know* you want to do good things. Sometimes.'

'Is this true?' Grandma said. 'You're *really* not from the Council?! Because that's—'

'Illegal,' Sima finished, staring at me. 'It's illegal, and it's . . . wrong. I am *so* sorry.'

'*Mr Stringer*,' my mum was saying, voice trembling, as I climbed the stairs, 'I'm sorry if I hurt your feelings, but we *really* need that deposit.'

'You *say* you're sorry,' Mr Stringer began to reply, 'but—'

And then I opened the door. Mr Stringer looked to me with a smirk . . . then Grandma and Sima followed me in, and his smirk faded.

'Sima!' he snapped. 'Go back to the car!'

Sima didn't move. But she didn't speak either. She simply stared at her boss, frozen.

'Typical,' Dad muttered to my mum. 'If *we* spoke like that to someone from the Council . . .'

'She's not from the Council – are you, Sima?' my grandma said, stepping towards Mr Stringer.

'. . . No,' Sima said, quietly at first, then more resolute.

'No. Mr Stringer pays me to pretend I am, so unwanted tenants leave more quickly than he's allowed to force them to go.'

'*What?*' Mum said quietly. 'Mr Stringer, is that—?'

'*Ken*, dear,' Grandma interrupted, her smile broadening like a shark's. 'I *think* we can call him *Ken* now, can't we? *Because we're not going anywhere.*'

Mr Stringer was speechless. He backed away from my parents, my grandma, Sima. For a moment he looked past them all, and saw me. Then I turned, and walked back to my room.

I knew they'd be in there for a while.

I returned to my room, feeling tired, angry . . . and elated. Had we saved the flat after all? Had we *beaten* Mr Stringer?

'That's unreasonable, now, PLEASE!' Mr Stringer shouted from the living room. For the first time ever, he sounded scared. They would probably be in there shouting at him for a *long* time.

I looked down at the track that had helped us, *the Infinite Race*. The amazing adventures we'd had in just a few days went through my mind. Winning a race. Escaping a merciless copper. Meeting *aliens* on a moon of Jupiter. Flying a horse across the eye of a storm.

It wasn't what he meant. But when Yamnaya said that the precious gems and gold he gave us were worthless compared to adventures, and games, and *friends*, he kinda had a point.

'Mr Green, I implore you!' Mr Stringer begged from next door. '*MRS GREEN, BE REASONABLE!*'

Yup, they'd definitely be there a while. I *probably* had time for a quick visit. I just needed to get . . .

Before that thought could finish, there was a knock at my door. I opened it, and there she was. My little sister, bothering me when I didn't want to be bothered, annoying me with all the things she copied off me, annoying me with all the things she did different.

I was so lucky to know her.

'What's happening?' asked Celestine. She was still red-eyed, but she was determined too.

'Good news, I hope,' I said, and pointed to the track. 'Cars or horses?'

That's when I saw the model tigers in her hand.

'You have GOT to be joking.'

Celestine just grinned.

Acknowledgements

Thanks first and foremost to Davinia Andrew-Lynch of Andlyn Literary Agency, for the advice, notes, belief and agenting. Thanks also to the Bloomsbury team, who brought stuff out of the story I didn't even know was there, especially illustrator David Wilkerson, who got so much heart and epic scale on the page, and my editor, Hannah Sandford, for notes that always pushed me in the right direction.

Thanks to the people who've encouraged my writing all this time. My parents and my sister Corinna are first on that list. Mum, you've got a mega sense of humour, and I'd like to think it's rubbed off. Dad, you've read pretty much everything I've ever written, and always found positives even when you weren't feeling it. I'll forever owe you your notes, racecar rotavator, and all the riddles I used to moan about but secretly loved.

Likewise, my In-Common-Laws David and Jean have become a second family. Jean, I swear that Kyan's grandma is a completely fictitious character, who just happens to be sternly there for the family throughout every crisis . . .

Chris and Lanna Bateman supported me years before I started all this nonsense. Much love, and don't you godkids Chas, Cal and Con ever think you'll escape my endless questions about yoof stuff. ('Do you still say "safe"? Is Fortnite still big?')

The same goes for Ashley Belgrave (not about the yoof trends, old'un, ha!). Thanks for your friendship and advice, from social media stuff back to how a scene properly moves (Go it, Shiftwork!). Thanks to Paul Hunter for the knock-out effects you provided for the book trailer. Please let's work on something together again. There's loads of other friends who've been supportive too – Ike, Claire, Steve, Nat, Krystal, Raj, Dave and Hugo, to name but a few.

I also wanna thank the people I work construction with. None of you ever sneered about my dream job. That counts for a lot. And yes, I am aware I'll be ripped for getting soppy now.

Lastly, but far from leastly (is that a word?), my family. D, you're my partner and best friend in every sense. Flipping heck our life's been hard, but you've made more sacrifices than me to get through it. I love ya more than ever, even though I know you'll use that last line the next time we argue (tomorrow).

And then there's the grotbags, the kids. Arf, Leo and Roobz. None of you have ever asked for those nicknames, and if you complained about them I probably just told you to BUCK UP. But I couldn't be prouder of any of you. Thanks for the laughs, the rows, Just Dance, music, and doing your chores. I love you all very much.

(Cue your awkward looks as your dad ahems and stares into the middle distance with watery eyes.)

Look out for

KYAN GREEN'S

next epic adventure!

Whizzing your way
Spring 2023

Colm Field gets called 'Colin' a lot. He doesn't help himself by mumbling his words a lot of the time, except in his job as a builder, when he winds up shouting instead. He lives in London with his three kids and his partner. Colm is happiest when he's excitedly writing a new story on his rusty old phone and his favourite mode of transport is walking, so obviously his debut children's novel is about high-speed multiverse-hopping on everything but feet.

David Wilkerson is a Black American illustrator who was born in Denver and is currently based in Maryland. He believes that there is healing in storytelling, and that it is the job of creatives to contribute to that cause. His career began in the animation industry and he has worked as a designer on various projects for clients such as Hulu and Cartoon Network.